Three Girls
in the City
SELF-PORTRAIT

By Jeanne Betancourt

D0094674

SCHOLASTIC INC.
New York Toronto London Auckland Sydney
Mexico City New Delhi Hong Kong Buenos Aires

Trademarks used herein are owned by their respective trademark owners and are used without permission.

No part of this publication may be reproduced in whole or in part, or stored in a retrieval system, or transmitted in any form or by any means, electronic, mechanical, photocopying, recording, or otherwise, without written permission of the publisher. For information regarding permission, write to Scholastic Inc., Attention: Permissions Department, 557 Broadway, New York, NY 10012.

ISBN 0-439-49839-2

3 4 5 6 7 8/0

12 11 10 9 8 7 6 5 4 3

Book design by Joyce White.

Printed in the U.S.A.
First printing, June 2003

ACKNOWLEDGMENTS
First and foremost, thank you to Maria Weisbin, my editor. Maria and Kate Egan were the original Girls in the City. Thank you also to Nicole Betancourt, Olivia Branch, Paul Greenberg, Teri Granger Martin, and Manuela Soares for their insightful reading of the manuscript.

TABLE OF CONTENTS

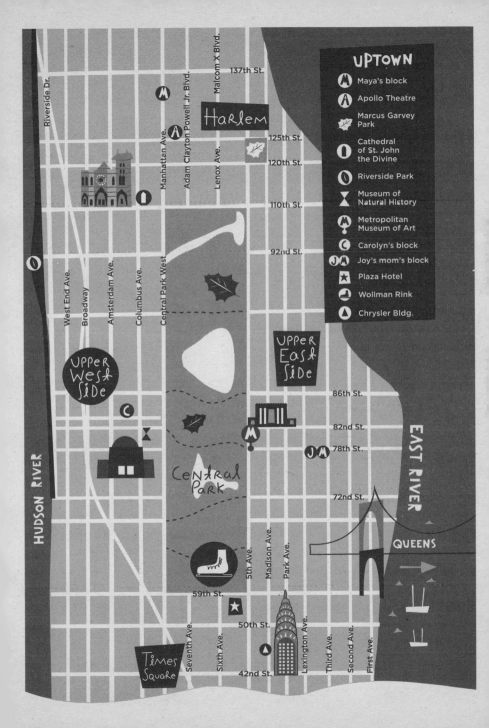

East Village

A week ago, Carolyn Kuhlberg was riding a horse across open fields. Now she rode a subway car stuffed with strangers who stood so close she could smell their breath. Her grandfather had warned, "In New York, they pack folks in those subways like sardines in a can." She'd tell him that the subways weren't always packed, mostly just at rush hour.

Carolyn climbed the stairs out of the subway tunnel with her father. Outside, the sky over New York City was as bright blue as any in Wyoming. But in New York, she'd noticed you only saw a little bit of sky at a time because of all the tall buildings. Back home, the sky went on forever.

They stopped at a corner and waited for the traffic light to change to WALK. Four cabs swooshed by. The driver of one wore a white turban. Is he from India? she wondered. Or is he from some country I've never heard of? She read the corner street signs. Eighth Street and Third Avenue. The photography workshop was on Eighth Street between Third and Second avenues. It would be in the next block.

Sooty smoke puffed from the backside of a

passing truck and blew in her face. Carolyn's father put his hand on her elbow. "Come on," he said as he steered her across the intersection. "We have the light."

A guy with short-cropped bleached hair streaked purple crossed in front of her. For a split second their eyes met and he nodded. How many piercings does he have on his face? Carolyn wondered. After he passed she remembered two in the nose, one in the eyebrow, and one on his lip. A total of four. What about his ears? He probably had a bunch of earrings there, too. She wished she could look at his face again.

A tall, dark-skinned woman in a long brown-and-bright-orange print skirt and matching headwrap was crossing the avenue in the opposite direction. She was pushing a stroller and rushing to get across before the light changed. The woman and her baby had the blackest skin Carolyn had ever seen. Have they just moved to New York City? she wondered. Do they feel lost like I do? Or are they native New Yorkers, born and raised here, who know exactly where they're going?

Carolyn and her father reached the other side of the intersection. Long, curling threads of sweet-smelling incense rose from a display of incense sticks and bottled oils on a small table. A guy with dreadlocks stood behind his wares, mumbling as he inched a string of wooden beads through his fingers. Carolyn wanted to stop and smell the different incenses and maybe buy some. Incense might cover up the new paint smell in their apartment.

They passed an Asian man arranging fresh flowers in white plastic buckets on the sidewalk in front of a deli. A pretty young woman in running shorts jogged out of the store carrying a bottle of water.

Carolyn quickened her pace to keep up with her long-legged father. He was in a hurry. After he dropped her off at the workshop, he had to take the subway back uptown to his job at the American Museum of Natural History.

Carolyn wondered if they'd be taking pictures on the street for the workshop. The incense man would make a good subject for a photo, she decided. So would the woman and baby with the beautiful dark skin. Would she have the nerve to ask the guy with all the rings and studs in his face to pose for her? That boy had a stud in his lip. Did it get in the way when he ate? How would it feel if he kissed you?

"Are you paying attention to where we are, honey?" her father asked. "We just crossed Third Avenue. The Youth Media Center is between Second and Third avenues."

She smiled up at him. "I know."

They passed three women carrying grocery bags and speaking rapidly in Spanish.

People from all over the world live in New York City, thought Carolyn. Would the other kids in the workshop be as different from one another as the people on the streets?

Carolyn had on blue jeans, a pink halter top, and a short-sleeved white shirt that she wore open. Her shoulder-length red hair was held back with a blue headband. The gold pony earrings her mother had given her hung from her pierced ears. Carolyn thought she looked okay when she left the apartment. Now she wasn't so sure. Everyone said kids in New York grew up faster than other places in the country. What if all the other kids in the class were really sophisticated? Would they think a kid from Wyoming didn't know anything? What did that song about New York City say? "If I can make it there, I'll make it anywhere." What if I *can't* make it there? Carolyn worried.

"You scared?" her father asked.

"Of course not," Carolyn told him. "It's just a class."

"Next stop, Eighth Street," announced the mechanical subway voice. Maya Johnson closed the newspaper she'd been reading. She'd taken two trains for a total of sixteen subway stops. I'll be spending a lot of time underground this summer, she thought.

It was her grandmother's idea that she should take the photography workshop. Even though Grandma Josie was retired from being a school principal, she knew about all the summer programs for kids in the city. Maya's three younger sisters were enrolled in activities, too.

"I checked your chart, dear," Grandma Josie had told her. "The stars are perfectly aligned for creative activity. It's a time for Aquarians to try new things. The photo workshop in the East Village is perfect for you."

When Grandma Josie's advice came from the stars, there was no point in arguing.

Maya loved the photos her grandfather used to take of the family. He'd catch those candid moments that showed you the way you really were. She knew that her grandfather had wanted to be a professional photographer. "Like Gordon Parks," he'd told her. But there weren't many jobs in the field for African-Americans when he was a young man coming up. My grandpa was a bus driver who wanted to be a photographer, thought Maya. I'm not going to let that happen to me. I'm going to find a way to make a living at something I love to do. She didn't know if that would be photography, but she was willing to try it.

Maya's father gave her Grandpa's reflex camera. "We need a new family photographer," he'd said.

Maya had practiced using the camera by taking two rolls of film at the family Memorial Day picnic at Jones Beach. Everyone said the photos were great. When her grandmother saw them, she smiled, raised her right eyebrow, and gave one of Maya's braids a little tug. It was her way of saying, "I told you so."

The train lurched to a stop. Maya stood to get off. "Step aside and let the passengers off," chimed the mechanical subway voice. She checked her watch. 9:55. I'll have to leave a little earlier in the mornings, Maya decided as she left the train in the crush of rushing New Yorkers.

She put her newspaper on the edge of the trash bin so someone else could read it. A white boy with purple streaks in his bleached hair and a lot of hardware in his face picked it up. He flashed her a quick thank-you smile. Maya nodded and turned toward the exit.

He's cute, thought Maya. But why'd he put all that metal in his face? Peer pressure? Rebellion? It'd be fun to take pictures in one of those piercing parlors. Show it like it is. A little blood and wincing. Her best friend, Shana, was a good example of what not to do in the piercing department. Her belly button became majorly infected. Swollen, red, and icky.

If I did a photo essay about piercing, Maya decided, I'd show that part of it, too. Why did people let themselves be yanked around by the *everybody's-doing-it* thing?

She ran up the stairs to the street. The light was green for walk, but she ran across and up most of the next block.

A vendor was selling incense and oils on the corner of Third Avenue and Eighth Street. "Do you have sandalwood?" she asked as she passed. He nodded. If he was still there after her class, she'd get some. But there wasn't time now. She didn't want to be late on the first day. What she really needed now was a cold drink. She spotted a food vendor on the next block. As she hurried down the street, she wondered who else would be in the workshop.

*   *   *

Joy Benoit-Cohen could walk to the photography workshop from her father's apartment on West Broadway or take the subway uptown two stops. Or . . . a cab turned the corner. Joy stepped off the curb and raised her arm to signal the driver to pick her up.

She threw her backpack into the backseat before flinging herself in headfirst and told him to take her to Eighth Street between Second and Third avenues. Through the cab's speaker, the tap-dancing Radio City Rockettes reminded Joy to fasten her seat belt. She didn't. When the famous opera star Jessye Norman or the playwright Wendy Wasserstein told her to "Buckle up for safety," she would. But not for the Rockettes, she thought. Not unless I'm with Mom, who'd make me buckle up. Dad — he wouldn't even notice.

The cab stopped for a red light. An African-American woman in some kind of orange-and-brown traditional dress pushed her baby's stroller across the street. If I wasn't taking this photography workshop, I'd be pushing a stroller all summer, Joy thought. Ugh! She hated baby-sitting for her baby half brother. I don't hate *him*, she decided. Jake was just a helpless kid. But she wasn't one of these girls who liked to baby-sit. Why did her father and Sue think she'd suddenly like baby-sitting because it was for her half brother?

After the baby was born, her father stopped introducing her as "my daughter, the Joy of my life." Now he said, "This is our daughter, Joy. The live-in baby-sitter." Her stepmother, Sue, introduced her that way, too.

"Excuse me," she'd wanted to say. "First of all,

I'm not Sue's *daughter*. Secondly, I only live with my father and his wife and their son *half* the time, which is hardly live-in. And thirdly, I'm *not* their baby-sitter." Instead she'd say, "Nice to meet you."

Joy wondered what the other kids in the workshop would be like. I won't know anyone there, she thought. She felt for her new digital camera through the soft leather of her backpack. Her mother had insisted that she have a good camera for the course. Joy had read the manual and knew how to use the camera. But there wasn't anything she wanted to take pictures of.

Maybe I should have the cabbie bring me up to Mom's apartment, she thought. Mom will be at work, so I'll have the place all to myself.

Joy imagined picking up a second breakfast at the café on the corner — a large moccachino and a jelly doughnut. She'd curl up on the love seat in her bedroom and watch old movies on TV. At lunch, she'd order in Chinese food. I'll take pictures of the doughnut and the takeout containers, she decided. Then if Dad and Sue ask what I did in class, I'll show them the photos on the computer screen and say the teacher had us photograph food. She'd have to remember to put out the garbage when she left, so her mother wouldn't know she had been there.

Before Joy could tell the cabbie to continue uptown, she remembered Ms. Sandler. She was the hitch in Joy's perfect-day plan. Ms. Sandler lived across the hall from Joy's mother and worked at home. At first, Joy thought it was cool having a famous mystery writer as a neighbor. But Ms. Sandler kept close tabs on the comings and goings on the twentieth floor and was a tattletale.

"Where on Eighth?" the cabdriver asked, snapping Joy from her daydream of playing hooky.

She looked out the window. They'd reached the intersection of Eighth Street and Third Avenue. No way did she want the other kids in the class to see her getting out of a cab. They might think she was some spoiled rich kid. She wouldn't tell them she went to a private school, either. Sometimes, the less that people knew about you the better.

"Right here is fine," she told the cabbie. She reached into her bag for her wallet as he pulled up to the curb.

"Looks like we've reached the end of the line," the tapping Rockettes announced as she handed him three dollars. "We'll see you at the Music Hall."

"Oh, shut up," mumbled Joy.

"I gotta listen to those dames all day," complained the cabbie.

Joy stepped out of the cab and called back over her shoulder, "Sorry about that."

She was checking the building number on the deli, so she didn't notice the table of incense sticks and bottled oils. Her backpack swung against it and bottles clinked and toppled against one another.

"Watch it, you cow!" growled the street vendor as he steadied the table.

Hoisting her backpack over one shoulder, Joy quickly moved down the street. She wished she'd dumped that guy's whole table on the ground.

She wished she'd had the nerve to go back and do it.

She wished she weren't on her way to a photography workshop with a bunch of strangers.

Maya rushed into an old stone building. She hoped that the first class would start a little late. An old security guard stood at a gray metal desk facing the door. "Sign in here," he said, turning a roster toward her. Maya scrawled her name under the heading PHOTO WORKSHOP I. Meanwhile, the guard looked through her backpack. A familiar wave of sadness washed through Maya. Whenever her bags were checked she remembered the terrorist attacks on September 11.

"Downstairs," the man directed.

As she headed down the stairs to the basement, Maya heard, "This is a hands-on workshop. So let's get to it." The workshop was already in session. She was late.

Maya walked in and flashed her biggest hello-I'm-here smile at the instructor. She felt the eyes of the other kids turned on her, but she maintained her cool. "Sorry I'm late," she said confidently. "Subways." Now she looked around at the other kids. "I'm Maya John —"

The instructor put up a hand to stop Maya. "Hold on. We're doing introductions later." She held out a Polaroid camera for Maya. "We're taking photos of each other. You'll be in pairs."

Maya took the camera, sat in the last vacant seat at the long wooden table, and glanced around. There were ten others — mostly girls — every other one with a Polaroid camera. Maya noticed two other black girls at the opposite end of the table. One had Rasta braids and wore camouflage pants. Maya tried to make eye contact that said, "Let's be partners," but the sister was fiddling with her camera. Anyway, the workshop leader was partnering kids with the person to their right.

Carolyn Kuhlberg couldn't take her eyes off the beautiful African-American girl who'd come in late. That girl is so confident, she thought. If I'd come late on the first day of the workshop I'd have died of embarrassment. Carolyn wondered how old that girl was, where she lived, and what subway she took to get to the workshop.

"Come on," muttered the girl beside Carolyn.

Carolyn realized she'd been daydreaming in class — already.

The girl had stood up. Carolyn looked up at her, confused. "We're portrait partners," the girl explained. She said portrait partners like it was a disease. "Let's get this over with." The girl motioned with the camera. "Let's go to the back."

Following her, Carolyn said cheerfully, "I guess we can say what our names are now. Mine's Carolyn. Carolyn Kuhlberg."

The girl stopped and turned to her. "Joy," she said simply. She pushed her long black hair out of her eyes and held up the camera. "I'll take your picture first."

"Focus on what interests you most about the person," the instructor called out. Joy glanced in her direction. The cocky black girl who came in late was stuck being the instructor's partner. Better her than me, thought Joy.

Joy held the viewfinder to her eye and watched the redhead smile for the camera. She noticed that little gold horses dangled from her ears. What's with the earrings? she wondered as she moved in for a close-up. How old is this girl? *Ten?* And that smile. It couldn't be real. *Click.* A photo shot out of the camera.

Carolyn watched the picture develop. It was a close-up of the corner of her upturned mouth and a dangling pony earring.

Joy glanced at the photo over her shoulder. "Cute earrings," she said.

Carolyn blinked. Were all the kids in New York going to be sarcastic? She sighted Joy through the lens and moved back to get a full head shot. Just as she snapped the shot, Joy turned away from the camera. The photo slipped out and developed into a blurred image of Joy's hair. Did she move on purpose? wondered Carolyn.

"I'll take another one," Carolyn offered.

"Don't bother. I like this one."

On the other side of the room, Maya framed her

shot of the instructor, Beth Bernstein. Beth's dark hair was cut close to her face and she was about six feet tall. She's the instructor, thought Maya, the one with all the power. I'm going to make her look like a big deal. Maya bent to one knee and pointed the camera up. "Put your hands on your hips," she directed. *Click*.

While the portrait developed, Beth took Maya's photo.

"Don't smile," Beth instructed.

"I wasn't going to," Maya shot back. She wondered if she was going to like Beth. So far she didn't.

As soon as the picture was out of the camera, Beth went back to the table. "Okay, everyone," she announced. "You'll introduce yourselves now. Tell us your name, show us the photo your portrait partner took of you, tell us what you think the photo says about you and anything else you want us to know. You each have a minute."

Latifa and Charlene from Brooklyn introduced themselves first. Maya thought, Those are the girls I'll hang with during the workshop.

Carolyn introduced herself by saying she'd just moved to New York City from Wyoming.

"There's a surprise," commented Charlene.

More sarcasm, thought Carolyn.

Joy did her introduction last. It was the shortest of all. When she finished, she crossed her legs and swung her foot. Maybe Beth Bernstein would learn to leave her out of discussions. She checked her watch. It was only ten-thirty. An hour and a half more to fill.

Boring, boring, boring. Baby-sitting this summer might have been the lesser of two evils.

"Eleven photographers," said Beth. She met Joy's gaze. "Some already bored."

Joy stared back. She already disliked this arrogant instructor. Teachers could be such control freaks.

"But, nonetheless, here we are," continued Beth. "So let's check out any cameras you brought. Those that don't have one, I have some here I can lend you for the summer. They're not half bad."

One boy and one girl took cameras from Beth. Everybody else had brought their own. Joy watched as the other kids took cameras out of backpacks and purses. A few looked as expensive as hers. That girl — Mara, or whatever her name was — had a camera that looked like an antique. The nerdy-looking boy on her left had a digital camera. Joy finally took out her camera and put it on the table.

Carolyn glanced at it. "Is that digital?" she whispered.

Joy nodded.

"Wow!" said Carolyn. "It's really nice."

Joy didn't even look at Carolyn, much less say thank you.

She doesn't like me, thought Carolyn. I wonder if anyone here is going to like me. She missed her old friends.

"The first assignment is self-portraits," Beth told them. "You'll choose your favorite to share with the class." She held up a large book of photographs. "I have some examples of self-portraits by famous photographers to show you. We'll discuss these. Then we'll talk about your ideas on how to take a self-portrait."

For Carolyn, the next hour went by in a flash. She felt too shy to participate, but Maya didn't.

"You could have someone else stand in for you while you set up the shot," suggested Maya.

"Huh?" asked Charlene.

"Oh, please!" mumbled Joy.

Joy doesn't like anyone, thought Carolyn.

Latifa's hand shot up and she started explaining what Maya meant. "Someone can stand where you'll be. They take your place in the shot. You look through the lens. That way you set the shot just the way you want it. Then you switch places."

"And your partner snaps the self-portrait for you," added Maya.

"That's one way," said Beth. She glanced around at the eleven participants. "And one that I want you to try. You're to work with partners for this assignment, so you can stand in for each other."

Please don't have us working with our portrait partners, thought Joy.

Carolyn thought the same thing.

So did Maya. She didn't want to have to do this assignment with the instructor. She wanted to work with Latifa or Charlene. She shot up her hand and spoke. "Can we choose our own partners?"

"Don't worry, Maya," said Beth. "I'm not doing the assignment with you."

Everyone in New York is sarcastic, thought Carolyn.

"There'll have to be one group of three," continued Beth. "Maya, you work with Carolyn and Joy. The rest of you stick with your portrait partners."

Maya sighed.

Joy rolled her eyes.

Carolyn heard Maya's disappointment and saw Joy's exasperation.

"Spend the rest of the class figuring out how you're going to work together," instructed Beth. "And have your portraits ready for next Monday's class. I'll go around and see if you have any questions" — she pulled a cell phone from her bag — "in a minute." She flipped the phone open.

"You can work with Mara," Joy told Carolyn. "I'd rather work alone."

"It's *Maya*," said Maya, who'd come up behind them.

Joy turned to her. "Like Maya Angelou, the writer?"

"Something like that," answered Maya. She thought that Joy was way too negative for someone named *Joy*. She glanced over at Latifa and Charlene. Why couldn't I be a third with them? I do *not* like Beth Bernstein, she decided.

Carolyn caught a whiff of musty incenselike perfume from Maya. She wondered if the man selling incense was still on the street. She looked from Maya to Joy. They don't want to do the assignment with me, she realized. Neither of them.

Maya noticed that Carolyn's studied smile had disappeared. She thinks we're rejecting her, thought Maya. For an instant Maya felt what it must be like to be new to New York City.

"Where do you live?" Maya asked Carolyn.

"One twenty-four West Eighty-second Street," answered Carolyn. "It's near the Museum of Natural History."

Joy raised her right eyebrow. "We know where it is," she said.

"You three," said Beth as she closed her cell phone. "No one gets out of this just because there are three of you. Where're you meeting and when?"

Joy and Maya exchanged a glance.

"Don't know yet," said Joy.

"I'll be back to you," said Beth. She strode over to the other side of the room to talk to the boys.

"Could we meet at your place tomorrow, Carolyn?" asked Maya. "We'll do your self-portrait first."

"Okay," agreed Carolyn. Maya watched a small smile work up the corners of Carolyn's mouth.

Maya looked at Joy. "What about you?"

If I stay home tomorrow, the stepwitch will expect me to "play" with the baby or — worse — babysit. She nodded.

"How's ten?" asked Maya.

"Sure," agreed Joy.

Joy looked at her watch. "Class is over," she said, standing up.

Maya noticed her leather backpack. Designer, for sure. And that fancy digital camera. This is definitely a rich girl, decided Maya. I bet she goes to private school.

"I think someone's looking for you," Joy told Carolyn.

Carolyn turned around and saw her father standing in the doorway. When he caught her eye, he tapped his watch as if to say, "Time to go."

"Hello, Mr. Kuhlberg," Beth Bernstein called out.

Carolyn felt her face turn beet red. Now everyone knew that her father was picking her up like she was in nursery school.

As Maya left the building, her stomach rumbled, "Time for lunch." She'd go back to the food cart on the street. Maybe Charlene and Latifa would eat with her. But she could see that they were already at the corner. She couldn't run after them. That would be exceptionally lame.

Joy walked slowly from the East Village to the West Village. She didn't want to go home yet. Her stepmother was home in the afternoon and would want to know all about the class. Then she'd most likely say, "Why don't you take your brother to the park." Ugh!

Maybe she'd stop at Gray's Papaya for two hot dogs and a papaya drink. Trouble with that was where to eat. The counters were along the windows where everyone could see you. She hated that.

As Joy walked up the block, she came to a diner with outdoor seating. She noticed a boy with purple streaks in his short bleached hair reading the *Daily News* and drinking an iced coffee. What's he trying to prove with all those piercings in his face? she wondered. She went into the diner and found an empty booth facing the back.

Carolyn's father bought her a sandwich from the deli on the way to their building, where he'd drop her off. She told him that she'd be doing an assignment with Maya and Joy the next day.

"That's wonderful," he said. "You're making friends already."

Not really, Dad, she thought. But she didn't say it. He kissed her cheek and left.

The elevator doors closed and she went up to the apartment to eat her lunch and spend the afternoon alone.

Central Park

Carolyn's father glanced at the kitchen clock. Carolyn followed his gaze. Twenty minutes after ten. Maybe Maya and Joy wouldn't even come. Maybe it would be better if they didn't. "Your new friends are late," he commented.

"You can go to work, Dad," she said.

"I'll wait. You can't go off with people I haven't met."

He poured himself another cup of coffee and turned back to his newspaper.

Carolyn looked around the small room and thought of its many functions — living room, kitchen, dining room, study. The whole apartment — including the two small bedrooms and bath — would fit in just the kitchen at her grandparents'. She touched her earlobes. Today she had on pearl studs. She had wanted to wear the pony earrings for her self-portrait, but if Joy was going to be there . . .

The downstairs doorbell rang. Her father pushed the intercom button and asked, "Who is it?"

"Maya," came the answer over the intercom. He pressed the button to let her in. Before Maya reached the apartment, Joy rang the bell, so the two girls came into the apartment one right after the other.

Carolyn noticed that Joy was dressed all in black again — baggy black pants, baggy overshirt. Maya had on denim shorts and a tiger-print scoop-neck T-shirt.

Carolyn introduced them to her father.

He shook their hands as if they were business associates and said, "I am pleased to meet Carolyn's new friends."

Friends, thought Joy. You got that wrong, Mr. Kuhlberg.

Carolyn guessed what Joy was thinking. Embarrassed, she looked at the floor. She was afraid he was going to scold Maya and Joy for being late. But he had an even more interesting way of embarrassing her.

He started by saying that he had to go to work at the American Museum of Natural History, but that he had waited to meet them.

"What do you do at the museum, Mr. Kuhlberg?" asked Maya.

Carolyn cringed as her father enthusiastically told her "new friends" that he was an entomologist doing a special project on a rare species of large cockroach.

Carolyn saw Joy gulp down a laugh.

"Interesting," said Maya as sincerely as she could,

Carolyn thought Maya was being sarcastic and wished with all her heart that her father would just leave. But did she really want to be alone with these two girls?

Ten minutes later, her father did leave. But not before he reminded her of a "few rules for her new life in the city."

"You can only be out in the company of your friends," he began. "And when you're done, I'll come pick you up." He gave her his cell phone. "Call me whenever you move locations." And finally, "Don't talk to strangers."

Even Joy was beginning to feel sorry for Carolyn.

When Carolyn's father finally left, an awkward silence took his place

Maya looked around. "So. How do you like it in New York?"

Carolyn suddenly felt shy. "It's okay," she mumbled.

Joy looked around the small apartment, too. "Where do you want to do your self-portrait?" she asked.

"In my room, I guess," Carolyn answered.

Joy wondered what Carolyn's bedroom looked like and decided that it was probably all pastels. She was right. There was a pink-and-blue floral bedcover, shaggy pink pillows, and a poster of two white horses rearing up. Even the walls were painted a soft pink. "Pretty room," she told Carolyn. "Pretty and pink."

Carolyn knew that she was being sarcastic.

"I'll stand in for you, Carolyn," offered Maya. "Where do you want me?"

Carolyn posed Maya on the edge of the bed and framed the shot to include her bed stand. She was about to snap a picture when Joy said, "Hey, *you're* supposed to be in the picture. Not Maya."

I am *so* stupid, thought Carolyn. She handed the camera to Maya and took her place on the bed.

After Maya took the shot, she suggested that Carolyn change her position and snapped her from a different angle. Maya took three more photos of Carolyn — all in different poses.

Joy watched and thought, Maya certainly likes to be in control. She isn't taking *my* picture — ever.

Maya suddenly realized what she was doing. "Oops," she said. "Guess those last few weren't your self-portrait." She handed the camera back to Carolyn. "Sorry. I got carried away."

Carolyn took the camera. "That's okay. It'll give me more pictures to send to my grandparents."

Maya pointed to one of the photos on the bed stand. "These are your grandparents. Am I right?"

Carolyn nodded.

"And the horse?" asked Joy, picking up Tailgate's photo.

"He's mine," answered Carolyn.

"Yours?" exclaimed Maya. "You own a horse? Is it in New York?"

"He's at our ranch in Wyoming," explained Carolyn. "My grandparents breed and sell horses. It's like a family business."

Maya noticed that the third photo was of a red-haired woman dressed in western clothes. She had a broad, warm smile. That must be Carolyn's mother, she thought. I bet her parents are divorced.

"Everyone's in the family business except for your father," commented Joy as she imagined a giant cockroach saddled up.

"Right," agreed Carolyn. She didn't bother to tell Joy that her grandparents were her mother's parents, not her father's. Or that her mother had been one of the best Western riders in Wyoming. Or that if she didn't stop talking and thinking about her family, she would burst into tears of loss and homesickness.

She had to change the subject.

She turned to Joy. "Where do you want to do your self-portrait?"

"I did mine already," answered Joy — even though she hadn't. She didn't want to bring these two girls to either of her homes. Carolyn, she already saw, lived in a small, underfurnished apartment. And Maya, she'd learned yesterday, lived in Harlem. How good could that be? My family has so much money compared to theirs, she thought. Besides, I don't want to take pictures of myself. I hate how I look.

Has Maya already done her self-portrait, too? wondered Carolyn. Will they both go now, and I'll be left here alone all day?

Maya noticed Carolyn's worried look. If I bail, she thought, what will Carolyn do? She isn't allowed to go out alone.

"I definitely need help with my self-portrait," said

Maya. "I have a favorite place in the park where I want to do it. But I'll have to pick up some stuff at home first." She looked Joy right in the eye and challenged her. "You don't have to come if you don't want."

Joy thought about the nuisance baby at her father's. She didn't want to go home. And she didn't want to have to kill time on her own. She might as well kill time with these two. Besides, she was curious about where Maya lived.

"I'm not bailing," she muttered.

Carolyn called her father to tell him that she was going to Maya's and to Central Park.

Ten minutes later, the three girls were on the number 1 train, heading north.

Carolyn noticed that at each stop there were fewer white people on the subway and more dark-skinned people. By the time they got off at 125th Street, she and Joy were the only white people in their subway car.

Joy was surprised that Maya's street — and a lot of the streets they walked on — wasn't run-down the way she'd expected. She looked up at the four-story brown building that Maya called "my house." It was as beautiful and detailed as any townhouse she'd seen on the swanky Upper East Side.

"We live on the top three floors," Maya announced as they walked up the front steps. "My grandmother lives downstairs." She pointed to windows at ground level.

Joy was surprised by what she saw inside the

brownstone. There were fancy woodwork and fire-places in almost every room — including Maya's large, sunny bedroom on the top floor. The furniture was mostly wood, polished to a dark, satiny glow.

Maya opened her closet. It was packed with clothes. "My mother has a secondhand clothing store," she explained as she flipped through the hanging clothes. "So I have *way* too much stuff. But of course the one thing I need isn't here. We'll have to stop by the store." She swung around and smiled at Joy and Carolyn. "Let's make sandwiches. We can take them to the park."

Carolyn was surprised and pleased by Maya's friendliness. Joy thought it was a little over the top. Exhausting, actually. But she was hungry, so she followed Maya and Carolyn to the kitchen, where they put together tomato-and-cheese sandwiches.

"Do kids in New York seem different from your friends back in Wyoming?" Maya asked Carolyn.

Carolyn remembered the boy with the face metal. "We don't have much body piercing back home," she said. "I saw this guy yesterday — when I got off the subway. He had four metal things in his face. Plus, I bet, in his ears." She turned one of her own stud earrings full circle. "And he had a purple streak in his hair. Kids at home — the high school kids — might do the weird hair and maybe one piercing — but not four. Not in Dubois, anyway." She didn't say that the boy smiled at her. Or that she wondered what it would be like to kiss him.

Maya sliced a sandwich in half. "Did the guy you saw — with the four face piercings — did he have bleached hair? I mean, except for the purple streaks."

"Yes," said Carolyn, surprised. "How'd you know that?"

"I think I saw the same guy," said Maya. "He took my newspaper from the garbage."

Carolyn wrinkled her nose. "He took it out of the *garbage*?"

"It wasn't *in* the garbage," Maya explained. "It was on top of the can. I left it there in case someone else wanted to read it."

Joy saw a boy with purple streaks and facial piercings like a photo in her mind's eye. She looked from Carolyn to Maya. "Was this guy wearing a lime-green shirt? Sleeveless."

"Yeah," said Maya.

Carolyn nodded.

"Did you see him, too?" asked Maya.

"He was in this place I went for lunch yesterday. And he was reading the newspaper." She pointed the mustard knife at Maya. "Probably *your* newspaper."

"We all noticed the same boy," said Maya.

"Newspaper Boy," added Joy.

Maya grinned. "Cool coincidence. I love when things like that happen."

"Me, too," agreed Carolyn.

Joy didn't say anything, even though she thought it was an extremely odd coincidence that they had all seen the same guy — *and* figured it out.

Especially since the three of them had so little else in common.

A few minutes later, the three girls left Maya's house. A tall, gray-haired woman in a colorful long skirt and loose top was watering window boxes.

"Hi, Gran," said Maya.

Maya's grandmother said hello and nodded at Joy and Carolyn. "You must be the girls from the photography workshop."

Maya introduced Joy and Carolyn to her grandmother Josie.

Carolyn liked how Josie gave her hand a little squeeze when she shook it. It wasn't a formal handshake, like her dad's. It was warm and friendly.

"Come on in for a minute," Josie said invitingly.

"Gran, we've got a lot to do," protested Maya.

"Just for a minute," insisted her grandmother.

The first thing Carolyn noticed about Josie's apartment was that it smelled the way Maya had smelled the day before. Like incense.

Joy noticed the books. Neat piles of them everywhere. She wondered what they were about. But they passed quickly through the room with all the books and the kitchen with spicy food smells and went straight out to the garden.

"It's the season for the roses," Maya's grandmother announced. "And the herbs are coming along nicely."

"It's a beautiful garden," observed Carolyn. A colorful hammock caught her eye. How wonderful it would be to lie in that hammock.

Maya's grandmother turned to Joy. *"Joy,"* she said. "That name can be a burden. When is your birthday?"

Joy was taken by surprise by both the statement and the question. She glanced at Maya.

"Gran is an astrologer," she explained. Her neighborhood friends were used to her grandmother. Some of them liked her and some — Maya knew — thought she was way too weird. Nonetheless, her grandmother was a celebrity of sorts in Harlem. First, for being principal of an award-winning alternative public high school. And secondly, for being a gifted astrologer.

"I'm a Scorpio," Joy finally answered.

Josie nodded. "A Scorpio. That's a powerful sign. Scorpios go very deep into things. And they like their privacy, so I won't say any more."

Good, thought Joy, because I don't believe in that stuff.

"My birthday is August second," Carolyn volunteered without waiting to be asked. She knew that she was a Leo. She and her best friend, Mandy — a Pisces — used to read their horoscopes in the newspaper and watch to see if they came true. But Carolyn had never met a real-life astrologer before. She wanted to hear what this unusual woman with her rose-filled garden would say about her sign.

Josie studied Carolyn and smiled. "A Leo. Leos are very creative and can be very brave. I have a feeling your moon is in Cancer, so you're probably sensitive to those around you."

Carolyn wanted to hear what else Josie might say about Leos, but Maya said that they should go.

Back on the street, Maya announced that her mother's store was on 125th Street. "It's on the way to our subway stop. Okay?"

Joy half listened as Maya explained that she was going to do three self-portraits, to reveal three aspects of herself.

Carolyn was fascinated and asked questions about how Maya planned to do it.

"There's this skirt I saw at the store," she answered. "A flowy thing from the seventies. Very flower child. It'll be perfect for the shot of the peaceful, studious me."

Three selves, thought Joy, I can hardly stand having *one*.

The store's sign was in ornate script: REMEMBER ME. Joy and Carolyn followed Maya inside. The sound of jazz and the smell of woodsy incense welcomed them. Maya waved to her mother, who was buttoning the back of a yellow satin gown for a customer. She looked up and added a smile to her welcome.

While Carolyn helped Maya search the racks for the skirt, Joy walked around the store. Sequined jackets had their own rack. And there were a lot of other fancy clothes in what looked like great condition. Glamorous hats were perched side by side on the shelves of glassed-in cabinets. In another cabinet, row upon row of jewelry glittered on red velvet pillows.

Finally, Maya pulled out a gauzy tie-dyed skirt

and held it up so her mother could see what she was taking.

Her mother left the customer and came over, and Maya introduced them. Carolyn thought she was businesslike and only sort of friendly. She already liked Maya's grandmother better.

"Come by to shop anytime, girls," Mrs. Johnson said. "Maya's friends get an additional ten percent off." She looked Joy up and down. "You're built like me. I could help you."

Maya's mother and grandmother are both busybodies, thought Joy.

Mrs. Johnson went back to her client, and the three girls went out to the street.

"The gown that woman was trying on is so pretty," Carolyn commented.

"It was Jennifer Lopez's gown," Maya said casually.

"The singer?" asked Carolyn.

Maya nodded. "Lots of people in show business bring my mom their used stuff."

"Did you see Jennifer Lopez?" asked Carolyn. "Did you get her autograph?"

Joy rolled her eyes. Carolyn saw it. It's not just words that can be sarcastic, she thought.

"Nah," answered Maya as she led the way down into the subway. "It's no big deal."

During the subway ride, Maya checked through her bag. She had everything she needed. And she'd chosen a spot in the park that had a rest room. She could change her clothes for her different selves in there.

The B train stopped at 110th Street. "This is us," announced Maya. "Let's go."

Carolyn was dazzled by Maya's confidence and how well she moved around the city.

Joy, on the other hand, was tired of the whole expedition. The entrance to the park Maya had chosen was up a long flight of stone steps. Why couldn't Maya take pictures of herself at home? she wondered. Or in her weird grandmother's garden? Sweat dripped from under her arms and down her sides. She sat on a bench in the shade. Maya put the lunch bag and her bag of props next to her. "Watch this stuff, okay? I'm setting up the first shot."

"Miss Wyoming can stand in for you," Joy said as she pulled a paperback book from her backpack. "I'm going to read."

Carolyn looked around the park. Grass, trees, runners, people with strollers. It was so beautiful and peaceful and she was still in the middle of New York City. The cell phone rang. When her father heard she was in the park, he cautioned her about muggers. "Stick close to your friends," he advised.

Maya motioned for Carolyn to stand on the edge of the grass so she could frame her shot.

Joy opened her mystery novel. She read intently, but every once in a while she looked up. When Maya went to the rest room to change outfits, Carolyn sat on the bench next to her and looked around nervously. Finally, Maya was done with her self-portraits. Self-indulgent self-portraits, thought Joy.

"Let's eat," said Maya. "I'm starved."

A vendor was selling drinks near the bathrooms. Joy and Carolyn bought sodas. Maya bought water. They sat at a picnic table in a grove of trees.

When they'd finished eating their sandwiches, Maya looked over at Joy. "You have to do a portrait in the park," she said. "Even if you did other ones at home. It's such a great setting."

Joy shook her head no. She hated to be bossed around. And she didn't want to take pictures of herself. That — to her mind — was the most uninteresting subject in the world.

"The one you do here could be the best," insisted Maya. "You, too, Carolyn." She tossed their wrappers in the trash can. She wasn't taking no for an answer. "Joy, you first."

Suddenly, Joy had an idea for her self-portrait. If I do it now, she thought, the assignment will be done.

"Okay," she told Maya. "You stand in for me while I set it up, and Carolyn can take the picture." Joy walked to the edge of the grass and looked up at the sun. She directed Maya to stand in the middle of the lawn where she would create a long shadow. Next, she framed the shot on Maya's shadow.

"When I take Maya's place," she instructed Carolyn, "take the shot of my shadow, not of me." Joy showed Carolyn where to stand, then took Maya's place on the lawn.

Carolyn thought it was strange to call a photo of your shadow a self-portrait. It was like Joy didn't want anyone to know anything about her. She looked through the lens and focused on Joy's shadow. It was an interesting and original shot. *Click.*

"What-ja doin'?" a voice bellowed in Carolyn's ear. She swung around to face a tall, bad-smelling man in worn clothes. "Got a quarter for me, honey?" he slurred. "I'll sing you a song."

Carolyn backed away and looked around. What if the guy tried to steal Joy's camera? What if he hit her? What if he had a knife? A gun?

Maya was beside her in an instant. "Move on, man," she told him. And he did. She smiled at Carolyn. "He's harmless. Just some poor homeless guy."

After that, Carolyn wasn't in the mood to do a self-portrait. But Maya insisted. Carolyn quietly set up her shot at the edge of the grass with lots of trees in the background.

A few minutes later, the three girls walked to the top of the long stone steps and started the descent to the street. A flash of red was coming up the stairs. Carolyn's heart stumbled over a beat. Red hair. Familiar red hair. Mom!

A woman in jogging shorts reached them. She was the same height and build as Carolyn's mother, with the same unusual shade of red hair. The woman nodded at the girls and smiled at Carolyn — another redhead.

A wave of sadness washed through Carolyn. The broad smile and friendly eyes — just about everything about that woman had looked like her mom. But it wasn't.

Saint John the Divine

Carolyn followed Maya and Joy down the rest of the stairs to the street. Seeing the red-haired jogger had left her breathless. Everything about that woman looked like her mother. In Dubois, Wyoming, with a population under a thousand, she never saw anyone she'd mistake for her mother. But in a city of millions of people, she thought, someone is bound to look like her. The jogger even seemed to be the same height as her mom. Carolyn remembered how, when she was little, her mother would stand her on a chair so they would be the same height. "Someday you'll be as tall as me," she'd say. "You might even be taller."

I am almost as tall as you now, Mom. But you're not here.

When the three girls reached the street, Carolyn was still thinking about her mother.

Maya noticed Carolyn's sad expression. That guy in the park must have really frightened her, she thought.

"How big is Central Park?" Carolyn asked suddenly.

"It starts at Fifty-ninth Street," answered Joy. "And ends somewhere up here."

"A Hundred and Tenth Street," added Maya. "We're at a Hundred and Sixth now." She hitched her stuffed backpack over both shoulders.

Carolyn looked up Central Park West. "So we're near where the park ends," she observed. "Can we see it?"

"We saw it when we got out of the subway at a Hundred and Tenth Street," Joy said with irritation. "It just ends. No big deal."

Joy's negative attitude was getting on Maya's nerves. She looked over her shoulder at Joy. "Just be glad she didn't want to see the *beginning* of the park."

"If we walked to the beginning, we'd walk right by the Museum of Natural History," observed Carolyn. "Right?"

Joy walked up beside her. "Where your father is studying the fearsome cockroach," she teased, wiggling her fingers in Carolyn's face. "Cockroaches are *really* aliens, you know."

"And your father is on a secret mission to stop them," added Maya.

Carolyn grinned at the image of her father fighting a giant cockroach, like a prince slaying a dragon. The cell phone in her bag rang, startling her.

"Uh-oh," said Joy with fake alarm. "He *heard* us."

The three girls broke into spontaneous laughter.

"Sh-sh," pleaded Carolyn as she opened the phone. She tried to be serious when she said, "Hi, Dad."

"Are you still in the park?" he asked.

"We just left."

"You were supposed to call me," he scolded. "Where are you now?"

"We just came out of the park," she said.

"Where are you going next?" he asked.

Carolyn looked from Joy to Maya and asked, "Are we doing anything else?"

Maya had a sudden inspiration. Saint John the Divine was only a few blocks away. It was the biggest cathedral in America, her family's church, and a real tourist site. She figured Mr. Kuhlberg would probably love it if they brought Carolyn to a church.

Maya reached for the phone. "Let me talk to him," she said.

Carolyn's eyes widened, and she clasped the phone to her chest. What was Maya going to say? He wouldn't think it was funny to call cockroaches aliens. Her father took bugs — especially cockroaches — very seriously.

"It's okay," Maya assured her. "Give it to me."

Carolyn reluctantly handed Maya the phone.

"Hello, Mr. Kuhlberg," said Maya in her most respectful voice. "It's Maya Johnson. Since we're only a few blocks from Saint John the Divine cathedral, I thought we'd go there." She winked at Carolyn. "Okay?"

"Excellent," agreed Mr. Kuhlberg. "Let's see. It's

four o'clock now. I'll be at work until six. I could pick Carolyn up then. Where will you go after the cathedral?"

Who does he think I am? wondered Maya. The baby-sitter? "Then we're . . . we're going to . . . this Chinese restaurant for ah . . . dumplings or something." She looked at Joy and shrugged her shoulders.

Joy shrugged back. It was fine with her. She liked dumplings.

Maya told Mr. Kuhlberg where the restaurant was. He said he'd pick Carolyn up there at six. She handed the phone back to Carolyn.

The girls didn't talk much on the way crosstown.

Carolyn wondered why they were taking her to a church. It didn't seem like something kids would do for fun.

Joy thought the day was getting to be a major drag. She didn't like churches — the few times she'd been in them.

Maya was still annoyed that Mr. Kuhlberg thought she'd watch out for Carolyn all day.

Saint John the Divine towered over them. The girls walked up the stairs side by side.

Stairs in and out of the park, thought Joy. Stairs in and out of the church. I might as well have gone to the gym. That was one of the things her stepmother, Sue, nagged her about. "A little more exercise would make you feel and *look* so much better, sweetie," she'd say. Then she kisses me on the cheek as if she hadn't just insulted me.

Joy walked into the dimly lit cathedral. At least it was cooler in there.

Carolyn looked up and up and up until her gaze stopped where stone arches met in the ceiling. Being in the cathedral felt oddly familiar. But why? she wondered. Their church at home was a small building with average-height ceilings. She turned herself around to take in all the hugeness. Memories of the towering gray canyons back home filled and lifted her heart. That was it. The cathedral reminded her of being in the canyons. She felt at home for the first time since she'd arrived in New York.

Maya leaned toward her and whispered, "There are all these memorial altars on the sides. Come on — I'll show you."

Carolyn walked with Maya past huge treelike columns to an alcove off the side aisle. There was a large open book under glass on a lectern.

"That book is filled with the names of people who died of AIDS," Maya said. "Thousands of them."

Joy wondered if her uncle's name was in the book. Bret Benoit. He'd died from AIDS when she was just eight years old. Bret was her favorite uncle. When her parents separated and started joint custody of her, Uncle Bret said he wanted custody, too — that he should see Joy at least once a week. Both her parents agreed. It was one of the few things they agreed on. So once a week, her uncle took her out. During the winter, they had Chinese food or went to a movie. When the weather turned warm, they rode their bikes in Central Park and had hot dogs and ice-cream bars. One summer evening, he brought her to hear the New York Philharmonic play in the park. They'd had a fancy picnic with Uncle Bret's boyfriend, Carl, and watched the night sky from a blanket on the Great Lawn. The concert ended with fireworks. Uncle Bret had kept that part a surprise. When Joy was assigned to write a poem in sixth grade about a perfect moment, she'd written about that moment with Uncle Bret — the blanket, the full moon, the orchestra — then, suddenly, the bangs and pops of fireworks joining the orchestra for the finale. When Uncle Bret was too sick to go out, she'd visited him with her mother. He was the first person she knew who died.

The organ's deep blast startled Joy out of her memories. Maya was beside her. "Ready?" Maya asked.

As the three girls walked away from the AIDS memorial, they came to a towering upside-down cross of charred wooden beams held up by metal fingers.

"It's in honor of dead firefighters," said Maya. "The pieces came from a fire."

Photos of firefighters, notes, flowers, and candles clustered around the base of the cross. These, Carolyn knew, were to honor firefighters lost in the World Trade Center. She'd seen street shrines like that on television after 9/11. The organist continued to practice.

Maya knelt in front of the memorial and bowed her head. When she stood up, Joy and Carolyn silently followed her toward the exit.

They'd almost reached the big doors when Joy jumped back and yelped, "Watch out!" A three-inch cockroach darted between her feet and scurried behind a stand of candles.

The three girls looked wide-eyed at one another and rushed from the cathedral. They burst into laughter the instant they were outside.

On the street, workmen attacked the pavement with a jackhammer, car horns honked, a jet plane roared overhead. They crossed the street and found the restaurant. It was noisy inside, too, Carolyn noticed — with the clanking of plates and the chit-chatter of diners. Spicy smells steamed off the passing platters of food. They made her mouth water.

Joy asked Carolyn if she'd ever had Chinese food.

Carolyn didn't think Joy was being sarcastic, but she wasn't sure. "I've had it," she answered. "But I don't know how to use chopsticks."

When they were seated, Carolyn pulled the cell phone out of her bag. "I better call my dad."

"He said he'd meet you here at six," Maya reminded her. "You don't have to call him."

"He's probably still in his meeting," added Carolyn as she snapped the phone closed without making the call.

"With the alien roaches," teased Maya.

Carolyn laughed.

"And their itty-bitty laptops," added Maya.

Joy rolled her eyes as if to say, "Enough with the cockroaches," and looked back at the menu.

What's her problem? wondered Maya. She'd had enough of joyless Joy.

"Let's have two orders of dumplings," suggested Joy. "And maybe some sesame noodles." She looked up at Carolyn. "Do you like sesame noodles?"

Carolyn nodded, even though she wasn't quite sure what they were.

"If you like peanut butter, you'll like sesame noodles," commented Joy.

They placed their food order and drank sodas.

"Did that burned cross in the church come from the World Trade Center?" asked Carolyn.

The image of the fires and smoke came to Joy.

"That memorial was for twelve firefighters who died in 1966," answered Maya.

"But now I guess it's for the firefighters who died on September eleventh, too," added Joy.

Maya drew a cross in the sweat on her soda glass. "My father's best friend, Ted, died at the World Trade Center. He was a firefighter."

Carolyn remembered that Maya's father was a police officer. "Was your father there?" she asked.

Maya nodded. "He went as soon as the second plane hit. But by the time he got downtown, the towers had fallen. A lot of firefighters and cops he knew were missing. He stayed down there for two days and nights searching for people." She paused before adding, "He was going to funerals for months."

The food came and they each took a share. Joy held a dumpling between chopsticks and bit off half.

Maya expertly swirled noodles around her chopsticks. She noticed Carolyn watching her, not eating. "Noodles are the hardest," she said. "Just use a fork."

When the eating slowed down, Carolyn quietly asked, "Did you see it happen? On September eleventh."

"I was on my way to school," answered Maya. "People on the street were running around and crying and hugging one another. I went back home and watched TV all day at my gran's. Gran and Mom and me. We were so worried about my dad being down there. We took turns taking care of my sisters upstairs, because we didn't want them to see it." She paused. "My friend Shana and I wore only black clothes for three months." She turned to Joy. "Where were you?"

"I was getting ready for school — putting on my shoes. The first plane hit. I heard it. Then I —" She tapped her chopsticks nervously on the table and stared at the small red paper lantern hanging low over their table. "Then I saw the explosion from the second plane hitting the other tower. From my bedroom window. And the towers falling. And the people running. I face — I faced — them. The towers." She looked down at her plate and twirled the last of her sesame noodles around the chopsticks. "My stepmother was home, but my father was out of town on business."

"It must have been awful to see it in real life," said Carolyn.

"My stepmother was hysterical and in a total

panic," continued Joy. "She thought it was the end of the world. Her mother and sister came to help her with the baby and everything. As soon as I could, I got out of there and walked uptown to my mother's office. This gray ash was on the ground. Soft, powdery ash, and office papers were everywhere. People were like in a daze. Everyone was heading uptown."

Joy didn't tell Maya and Carolyn that she had kept her bedroom blinds closed ever since then.

"How did you find out what was happening?" Maya asked Carolyn.

"In Wyoming, it's two hours earlier than here," began Carolyn. "My grandparents were doing ranch stuff in the barn and heard about it on the radio. I was getting dressed for school when my grandmother told me."

The waiter cleared away their dishes.

"I guess you watched on television, too," said Maya.

Carolyn nodded. "The next day, there was a special service at church. My friend Mandy and I helped paint a big American flag on the side of our barn."

"What about your parents?" asked Maya. "Where were they?"

"My father was in Africa doing research — you know — on insects. And my mother —" Her throat tightened. "She — uh — died" — she rushed through the rest of the sentence — "just three months before that."

The waiter put a plate of quartered oranges and

cellophane-wrapped fortune cookies in front of them. The girls were quiet for a long time.

"I'm sorry about your mother, Carolyn," said Maya.

"Me, too," added Joy. "I guess that's why it's just you and your dad."

Carolyn nodded.

"I thought maybe your parents were divorced," said Joy quietly.

Carolyn shook her head.

Maya was lost for a moment, imagining life without her own mother. She couldn't stand the thought. How did Carolyn's mother die? she wondered.

Joy thought about how awful it would be to live with just her father.

Carolyn tugged at the cellophane wrapper on the fortune cookie.

At that instant, Maya saw Shana through the restaurant window. She was striding along, laughing and talking, with a few of their friends. As Shana glanced at her own reflection in the window, she saw Maya. Shana's surprised expression asked, "What are you doing with those two white girls?"

What *am* I doing with two white girls? wondered Maya.

Shana turned back to their friends and crossed the street. Maya wanted to run out of the restaurant and catch up with them. If Carolyn hadn't just told me her mother's dead, I would, she thought. If I wasn't practically baby-sitting Carolyn, I would. She turned to Carolyn and asked, "So what's your fortune?"

"'There is a pot of gold at the end of your rainbow,'" Carolyn read. "I guess that means I'm going to be rich."

"Mine says the same thing," said Joy. "But I don't believe in fortune cookies." She put the cookie in her mouth. It tasted like cardboard, but she ate it anyway.

Maya opened hers and read, "'Make new friends but keep the old.'"

"That's perfect," blurted out Carolyn. In the instant she said it, she wished she hadn't.

Maya crumpled up her fortune. "I don't believe in fortune cookies, either," she said.

Carolyn's eyes widened with hurt and embarrassment. Maya thought, Carolyn's way too sensitive for this city. "I don't mean people shouldn't make new friends," she explained. "I just think that the fortunes in fortune cookies are mostly lame."

"Yeah, me too," agreed Carolyn. She tied the wrapper from her straw into a knot. She wished her father would come get her. She wished she hadn't told these strangers about her mother.

On the way home, Carolyn's father asked her what she'd done with her new friends.

"They're not friends," she told him. "They're just girls from my photography class. Beth told us to work together."

"Miss Bernstein," he said, correcting her.

She didn't bother telling him that everyone in the workshop called her Beth.

He repeated his question, substituting "girls in your photography class" for "new friends."

Carolyn told him about her day, skipping the part about the homeless man who frightened her. As they were going into their building, she asked him about his day. When he told her that he was organizing an important international conference on cockroaches, she had to fake a cough to keep from laughing.

Maya walked uptown and dropped her roll of film off at the one-hour photo shop near her house. She wondered where Shana and the others went. She brought the skirt back to Remember Me and helped her mother put out some new old clothes that had come back from the dry cleaner that day. Then she headed back to the photo shop to pick up her prints.

When she got home, she laid her self-portraits on her bedspread. First pose: standing in a karate stance, hair held back with a red triangle scarf low on her forehead, baggie cutoffs, ripped black T-shirt. Shot from a low angle so she'd look threatening. The "don't mess with me" Maya. But I'm not one of those tough girls, she thought. And I hate ripped clothes.

Second pose: sitting on a park bench, hair pulled back, glasses, long skirt topped with a loose Indian blouse. The "studious, quiet, private" Maya. But I'm not the quiet, studious type, either. And I hardly ever dress that way.

Maya studied the photos of the last pose — a

medium shot of herself leaning against a tree in her favorite denim shorts and a sleeveless animal-print T-shirt. Her hair was loose, but pulled back off her forehead. That's the real me, she thought. The African-American "here-I-am-this-is-me" me. Maybe I should have stayed uptown this summer and been an assistant counselor at The Kids' Place Day Camp with Shana. Maya squared off the photos and put them back in the envelope. She decided she wouldn't spend any more time with Carolyn and Joy. Today had been a mistake. From now on, she'd do stuff with her real friends.

Joy took her time getting home. When she finally went into the apartment, she heard baby giggles and squeals from the living room. Her father was tossing baby Jake in the air and shouting proudly, "There's my big boy. The best baby in the world." Sue was shrieking, "Oh, Teddy, be careful."

Joy went to her room, downloaded the photos of her shadow into her computer, and opened the file. A lengthened human shadow slashed across the screen. That's it, she thought as she studied the photo. That's my self-portrait. She spun the desk chair around with her foot. It came to a halt in front of the closet door mirror.

I hate how I look, she thought. I already have old-lady lines on my forehead. And I'm fat. She stuck out her foot and kicked the mirror before swiveling back to the computer.

*   *   *

Carolyn's father opened his laptop on the counter separating the kitchen from the living room. She went to her room, closed her door, and sat on the edge of her bed. It was only 6:30. It would be light out for another two hours, but she couldn't go out alone, not even to the corner store to get gum or something. Back home, she had total freedom, and there was always something interesting to do on the ranch. Sometimes, on a summer evening, her mother would tell her and her friends to saddle up and she'd take them out for a moonlight trail ride.

Carolyn remembered how Joy thought her parents were divorced. My parents were different from each other, she thought. Mom was relaxed and fun-loving. Dad is kind of strict and serious. If Mom hadn't died, would they have divorced? If they had, I would most definitely have lived with Mom.

Mom.

She looked around her room for something to stop the familiar, awful rush of sadness about to sweep over her. Maybe she'd write a letter to Mandy and tell her about her first week in New York City. But what exactly would she tell Mandy? *Everything* was different from home. Maybe she'd just send her a postcard. She riffled through a small stack of cards on her bedside table and picked out one of the Statue of Liberty. She turned it over and wrote: MANDY: NEW YORK IS INTERESTING, FUN, AND VERY NOISY. I'M MEETING NEW PEOPLE BUT I MISS YOU. LOVE, CAROLYN

She went over to her bedroom window and faced the yellow brick wall of the next building. She remembered the view from her window at home. There, she looked out over fields that didn't end until — in the far distance — they reached the foot of the snowcapped Teton Mountains. Tears spilled down her cheeks. She threw herself across her bed and covered her head with a pillow so her father wouldn't hear her cry.

Greenwich Village

Maya watched her flickering reflection in the subway window. She'd spent all of the day before with Shana. They went to Jones Beach with the day campers from The Kids' Place and hung out in the evening with Delores and Jay-Cee. Shana didn't mention seeing Maya in the Chinese restaurant. Neither did Maya.

As the train slowed to a stop at the Eighth Street station, Maya tucked the newspaper under her arm and moved toward the door. I'm definitely going to sit at Latifa and Charlene's end of the table today, she decided. I want to hang with them, not Carolyn Cowgirl and Joyless Joy.

As Maya came out of the car, a flash of purple-streaked blond hair caught her eye. She pressed up to her tiptoes and peered over the crowd. Newspaper Boy was moving toward the train she'd just left.

He saw her.

She placed her newspaper on the nearest trash can and turned toward the stairs. After a couple of steps up, she glanced back. He had her paper. He is Newspaper Boy, she thought with a grin.

He grinned back at her before slipping sideways between the closing doors of the subway car.

A man in a suit pushed past her, his briefcase knocking against her leg. "Make up your mind," he grumbled. "You goin' up or down?"

"Sorry," she said as she ran past him up the stairs.

Maya was still thinking about the boy when she bought an orange juice from a food cart. There was something odd about Newspaper Boy's grin. What was it? She suddenly laughed, "Ha!"

"My juice is funny?" the food vendor asked. "Something, perhaps, is wrong with it?"

"No, no," protested Maya. "The juice is great." She ran down the street. She couldn't wait to tell Carolyn and Joy what she'd learned about the boy they'd all noticed the first day.

Joy took a cab to the workshop, but she was still late. "Let's check out your self-portraits," Beth was saying when she came in. "First, we'll tell you what we see in your photos. Then you can tell us what you were after by way of expressing yourself."

Joy looked around for an empty seat. She wasn't surprised to see Maya sitting with Latifa and Charlene. The only empty seat for her to take was between Carolyn and Nerdy Boy. Carolyn moved her chair over to make more room. She did that because she thinks I'm fat, thought Joy. She glared at Carolyn before sitting.

Carolyn turned away from Joy's hard look. Why doesn't she like me? she wondered.

Maya was the first in the workshop to talk about her self-portrait. Carolyn was surprised that she showed only one of her poses — the one in front of a tree. It was because of the tree that Latifa commented that Maya probably had a house in the country. The boy sitting next to Joy, whose name Carolyn couldn't remember, thought that the tree symbolized strength and being rooted. Carolyn thought his comment was interesting.

So did Maya. "I didn't think of that symbolism when I decided to put the tree in my self-portrait," she explained. "But I do see myself as independent. That's why I'm standing alone." She smiled at Latifa. "I don't have a country house, but I love nature, which is why I'm in one of my favorite parts of Central Park."

Charlene was the first to comment on Carolyn's self-portrait. "Who are all those people in the pictures behind you?" she asked.

Carolyn wished she hadn't included the snapshot of her mother in the self-portrait. She didn't want to talk about her. She felt a blush blossom on her cheeks.

Maya noticed her embarrassment. "I think those photos say that Carolyn loves her family and horse," she said, so Carolyn wouldn't have to answer Charlene's question. "She's connected to her family, even though they're thousands of miles away." She looked over at Carolyn. "Am I right?"

"Yes," agreed Carolyn. She smiled a thank-you at Maya.

Charlene looked over her glasses at Maya. "Maya girl," she scolded, "you only know that because you're in the same group."

Joy was the last one to share her self-portrait. A few people thought that photographing her shadow was a cop-out. All Beth said was, "I'm curious to see how you'll handle the rest of the assignments."

After that, Beth announced a short break.

Maya watched Latifa and Charlene leave the room without inviting her. At the other end of the table, Joy pushed her chair back and looked bored. Carolyn was writing in her notebook. Maya went over to them.

"Hi," said Carolyn shyly. "Thank you for showing me around yesterday."

Maya nodded. "That's okay. Guess who took my newspaper this morning?" She poked Joy on the shoulder to include her in the question.

Joy's head shot up.

"Guess," repeated Maya.

"Newspaper Boy?" Joy and Carolyn answered in unison.

Maya nodded. "He's got even more metal than we thought."

"More?" exclaimed Carolyn with alarm. "Where?"

"In his mouth," answered Maya.

"On his tongue?" asked Carolyn, sure that she was right.

"Newspaper Boy has braces," Maya announced. She was happy to have finally shared the news.

Even Joyless Joy grinned. "Braces!"

"Exactly. And he took my paper again," added Maya.

She propped herself at the edge of the table, facing Joy and Carolyn.

"He must have been waiting for you," said Joy. "It's too much of a coincidence."

"It's scary," said Carolyn. She looked up at Maya. "Isn't it?"

"No," she answered emphatically. "The guy's got braces."

Carolyn imagined her father's stern voice: "Whoever said people who wear braces can't be criminals?" She was glad she hadn't said anything to her father about Newspaper Boy.

"I bet he'll take your newspaper again," said Joy. "Let's leave him a message. In your newspaper."

"What will you say?" asked Carolyn. "You can't ask him why he's got so much metal in his face. I mean, can you?"

"That's too straightforward," said Joy. "The message should be offbeat, maybe sarcastic." She locked eyes with Maya. "Would you do it? I mean leave him a note in a newspaper?"

Maya thought the idea was a little childish, but still — "Sure," she agreed. "I — we — just have to decide what to say."

"Break up the break," Beth announced with a clap. "We've got a lot to do."

Latifa and Charlene came back into the room.

Maya stood abruptly and went to the other end of the table. She hadn't wanted Latifa and Charlene to see her with Joy and Carolyn.

During the next hour, Beth led a discussion on photographic techniques, using their self-portraits. Everyone had to say how they might have shot an even more revealing photo of themselves.

I hate this workshop, thought Joy. Everyone is saying such personal stuff. Like Nerdy Boy talking about how he wished he'd taken his photo out of focus because he has some weird vision problem that could make him blind someday. I feel sorry for him, but really! And Charlene saying she should have taken her picture near an overflowing garbage can because her neighborhood is poor and crime-ridden and people are treated like trash by the government. So take the picture, don't talk about it. Then that older girl, Janice, who couldn't stop yakking about her lesbian mothers, even though her self-portrait had nothing to do with that. Puh-lease, spare me the details. What do they think? That we're on *Oprah* or the *Jerry Springer Show*?

Beth used Janice as an example for the next assignment: Who is your family?

How am I supposed to take photos of my family? wondered Carolyn. My mother is dead and my grandparents are thousands of miles away.

"I hate this," mumbled Joy.

"Me, too," agreed Carolyn.

The more Beth talked about the assignment, the more annoyed Joy became. Finally, she spoke up. "You want us to talk about all this personal stuff," she said. "But you're not telling us anything about yourself. I, for one, don't think it's fair."

A couple other kids mumbled their agreement.

Carolyn felt nervous heat move up her face. She'd never heard anyone challenge a teacher like that.

"Joy, it's an unfair world," stated Beth flatly. "I also get paid to be here, which you don't," she added sarcastically. "Tough, isn't it?"

Joy pushed the hair out of her eyes and stared back at Beth.

"Later in the workshop you'll be doing photos about people other than yourself and your families," Beth continued. "But photographing what is familiar is the best way to begin. You have to trust me on this one."

No I don't, thought Joy.

Maya's hand shot up. "Could you bring in some of your photos, Beth? I'd be interested in seeing them."

Beth thought for a second. "Okay," she agreed. "I have a project in the works. It'd be interesting to get some feedback on it."

Carolyn was shocked by Joy's and Maya's boldness. She would never ask a teacher something like that, much less question or criticize one. And she hadn't used a teacher's first name since she was in nursery school. Is this what kids are like in New York City schools? she wondered.

At the end of the workshop session, Joy turned to Carolyn. "Let's get Maya to leave a message for Newspaper Boy," she said. "Come on. We'll help her write it."

They caught up with Maya at the door.

Carolyn hoped her father wasn't in the hall waiting for her. He wasn't. He wasn't in front of the building, either.

The three girls stood on the sidewalk, facing one another.

"Maybe we should just ask Newspaper Boy what his name is," suggested Maya, "and ask him why he takes my newspaper."

"That's too direct," said Joy. She turned to Carolyn. "Do you have any ideas of what to say?"

"What if it just said 'Have a nice day'?"

Joy grinned at her. "Great. That's got humor and irony."

"Humor?" said Carolyn. "What's funny about it?"

"What you just said is what makes it funny. That everyone takes it so seriously, but since everyone says, 'Have a nice day' — even to strangers — how sincere can it be? That's what makes it ironic."

"I see what you mean," said Carolyn — even though she didn't.

"Have a nice day," repeated Maya. "It's perfect."

She hiked her backpack on her shoulder. It was time to go back uptown. She'd say good-bye to Carolyn and Joy and —

"Where did you see Newspaper Boy the other day?" Carolyn asked Joy.

Maya waited to hear the answer.

"In the West Village," said Joy. "At this diner on Eighth Street. He was sitting outside."

"The Village?" asked Carolyn, confused.

"West Village," said Joy. "It's just crosstown from here."

"Haven't you been there?" asked Maya.

As Carolyn answered that she hadn't been to the West Village, she saw her father coming up the block. He motioned for her to meet him. "I have to go," she added.

Maya and Joy walked down the block on either side of her. Joy felt a little sorry for Carolyn. What was the point of living in New York if you couldn't hang out in the Village?

"I could show you now," Joy told Carolyn.

"Me, too," Maya added. "Then I can take the West Side train back home. I won't have to change." She looked at Carolyn. "We can take the same train — if your dad will let you go."

"We could have lunch," added Joy, almost without thinking.

Carolyn felt a surge of excitement. If only her father would let her.

Mr. Kuhlberg greeted them with a "Hi, girls. How are you today?"

Maya and Joy answered courteously.

"Do you have homework to do together again?" he asked.

"No," they all replied. They looked at one another, surprised that they had answered in unison.

"But we do have some workshop stuff we have to talk about," said Joy.

"So we wondered if we could have lunch together down here," added Maya. "Then — I'll go uptown on the train with Carolyn."

Mr. Kuhlberg looked directly at Maya. "She'll have to be home by three."

"Okay," agreed Maya.

"And you'll get off the train with her? And walk her to the building?"

As Maya nodded that she would, she thought, This guy is way too overprotective.

Carolyn was embarrassed that Maya had to take her home like she was her baby-sitter. Her father even offered Maya money for the extra train fare because she had to get back on the train to go home herself. Maya told him she had a weeklong pass, so it wouldn't cost any more. Next, he reminded Carolyn to call him when she got home.

When he finally left them, he called over his shoulder, "Have a nice day."

Carolyn and Joy exchanged a grin.

"You're right," said Carolyn through a giggle. "It *is* funny."

Maya was amazed at how happy Carolyn was about staying downtown. It doesn't take a lot to make her happy, she thought. "Let's get sandwiches at a deli and eat in Washington Square Park," she suggested.

"Okay," agreed Joy, though she really preferred to go to an air-conditioned café.

Carolyn wondered if the park would be as big as Central Park.

It wasn't even close. From where they ate their sandwiches, Carolyn could easily see the streets surrounding the park. And a person could walk from one end of the park to the other in a few minutes.

After lunch, they wandered in and out of stores on Eighth Street. The stores mostly sold posters, incense, and T-shirts with pictures of music stars and actors and sayings like "Save the Planet" and "Groovy, Baby."

Carolyn noticed that there were a lot of kids with tattoos and pierced skin hanging out in this neighborhood. She looked for braces on other kids with piercings. She didn't see any, but then, she noticed, the kids with a lot of piercings and tattoos didn't smile much.

"I hate all those head shops," commented Joy as they crossed a busy intersection. "They all have the same stuff and it's stupid."

A group of kids passed them going in the other

direction. They all had on baggy jeans and tight sleeveless T-shirts.

"I hate it when everyone dresses alike," said Maya. "I say wear what you want and be yourself."

Easy for you to say, thought Joy. You're an ideal size with gorgeous hair and all the self-confidence in the world. She hated how life could be so easy for some people.

They stopped to look in a shoe store window.

"How do the kids back in Wyoming dress?" Maya asked Carolyn.

"Like me," answered Carolyn. She was sorry the instant she said it.

"See what I mean?" said Maya. "Everyone dresses alike." She saw hurt wipe the smile off Carolyn's face. "It's okay," she continued, turning back to the store window. "Lots of people dress the same as lots of other people. It's the way the world is. I just hate how the media tries to tell us what to wear. You know, this year everyone should wear pointy-toe shoes with thin heels and the next year they'll tell you to wear square toes and thick heels so you'll buy all new shoes. Or how about baggy jeans? Now you're beginning to see more skintight jeans. It's all just to sell stuff."

"Don't you and your friends dress alike?" Joy asked Maya's reflection in the store window. "You said that you and your best friend wore only black after September eleventh."

"That's different," said Carolyn. "Isn't it?"

Maya turned away from the window and faced

Joy in person. "We didn't wear the same *style* black clothes. Besides, nobody told us what to do, like by advertising or something. But you're right in a way. Sometimes I wear stuff that's like what my friends wear. And sometimes they copy me. Still, I try to keep all those advertisers from influencing me."

Joy didn't want to talk about fashion and clothes anymore. What if they started talking about how *she* dressed in baggy clothes to cover up her fat? No one would want to copy how I dress, she thought. No danger of that happening. "I'm going home now," she announced suddenly. "See ya." She gave a little wave and left Maya and Carolyn standing — surprised — in front of the shoe store.

Maya checked the clock on the library tower. "It's already two o'clock," she told Carolyn. "We might as well go home, too."

Maya doesn't want to hang out with me anymore now that Joy's gone, thought Carolyn. As if to prove that Carolyn was right, Maya didn't talk much during the subway ride uptown. The train was crowded, so they stood facing each other, holding on to the same pole. It would have been easy to have a conversation. Maybe Maya's not talking because she's on the lookout for muggers and pickpockets like my dad always is, thought Carolyn. Or maybe it's because she's annoyed that she has to walk me home.

The doors to the train opened at 59th Street and a whole new crowd of people pushed in. A man grabbed the pole above Carolyn's hand. As the train jerked forward, he fell against her. She turned and their eyes locked for an instant. His eyes were tired and bloodshot. His hot breath bathed her face.

She let go of the pole and turned as much as she could away from him. Remembering that her wallet was in her backpack, she felt to be sure that the zipper was closed. It was. She was glad she was with Maya and not alone. Her father was right when he warned her that anyone could be a crazy. But Maya doesn't want to ride with me, thought Carolyn.

By the time they finally reached Carolyn's building, Maya was wondering how she could get out of being her chaperon.

"Good luck with the assignment this weekend," she said.

"Are you going to leave that note in the newspaper on Monday?" Carolyn asked.

"Maybe. Gotta go. See you on Monday."

"Yeah. See you. Have a nice weekend." Carolyn's hand shot to her mouth. "Oops. 'Have a nice weekend' is like 'Have a nice day.' Right?"

"Sort of," agreed Maya. She turned to leave and called over her shoulder, "You have a nice weekend, too."

I won't have a nice weekend, thought Carolyn as she walked into the lobby. What will I do with all the time between now and Monday?

Upper East Side

Friday would be changeover day for Joy and she'd be going back to her mother's on the Upper East Side for a week. Thursday night was her only chance to take pictures of the dad half of her family, which now included Sue and the baby.

Sue was flattered that Joy wanted to take her picture. "Make me look pretty," she said in her sweetest voice. "Where do you want me?"

"In your bedroom at your dressing table," answered Joy. "I'm going to take your picture looking in the mirror."

Just like the wicked stepmother in the fairy tale, thought Joy with secret satisfaction. "Mirror, mirror, on the wall, who is the fairest of them all?" As Joy followed Sue's slender back into the bedroom, she remembered that in the fairy tale, Snow White was the fairest, not the wicked stepmother. But in my story, the stepmother is the fairest, thought Joy. Sue Cohen — slave to fashion.

Sue sat at the dressing table. "I'll just do a little touch-up."

Joy looked through the lens.

Sue putting on earrings. Click.

Sue combing her hair. Click.

Sue applying lipstick. Click.

Sue smiled up at Joy and said, "I'm ready."

"That's okay," Joy told her. "I already got the shots I wanted. Thanks."

Next, Joy went to the living room where her father was reading a board book to Jake.

"Dad, I've got to take a picture of you and Jake for that workshop," she announced.

He grinned at her. "Terrific. I'll want copies."

Her smiling father cheek to cheek with drooling Jake. Click.

"Toss him up in the air like you did yesterday," directed Joy.

"Sure thing," her father agreed. "Jakey will love that." He stood and tossed the baby in the air.

Baby Jake suspended, his mouth wide open in surprise. Her father looking adoringly up at him. Click.

Jake squirming and crying in his father's arms. Click.

"He wants to fly some more, don't you, big boy?" her father cooed.

Another toss. Click.

"Thanks," Joy said, turning off the camera. "I got enough."

Friday morning, Carolyn went to the museum with her father. She wanted to take pictures of him in his office. He sat at the desk and looked serious.

"Smile, Dad," she instructed. "I want to show that you like your job."

"That certainly is true. I do like it." He picked up a hand-sized metal replica of a cockroach and grinned at the camera. "Take a picture of me with my research subject."

She took the photo. But no way — no way ever, ever, ever — would she show that photo to the class.

When they'd finished the photo session, Carolyn asked her dad if she could walk around the museum by herself. He agreed but insisted that she leave her camera and wallet locked in his desk drawer. "And don't talk to anyone."

Carolyn went directly to her favorite exhibit in the museum — the butterfly conservatory, where dozens of species of butterflies lived in a natural habitat. As Carolyn wandered around the exhibit, a black butterfly with a luminescent blue pattern landed on her arm. She stayed perfectly still. A woman pointed out the butterfly to a small boy and whispered to Carolyn, "I just love butterflies. Don't you?"

Carolyn smiled her agreement. The butterfly lifted off her arm and flew away.

"Butter flies," the little boy told Carolyn with a giggle.

"And jelly jiggles," she added.

"Jelly jiggles," repeated the boy with delight.

They watched the butterfly suck nectar from a purple orchid.

People in New York are so friendly, thought Carolyn. Why does my father think I shouldn't talk to anyone? She suddenly remembered the man falling against her on the subway. Was that man really dangerous? Would he have stolen her wallet if he had the chance? Or was he just a tired passenger trying to find space in a crowded train?

That evening, Carolyn sat on her bed and wondered what else she could shoot for the Who is your family? assignment. She'd already included photos of her mother and her grandparents in her self-portrait. She couldn't do that again. She picked up her mother's photo and studied it. Her mother, smiling confidently, dressed in her usual jeans and a plaid shirt, leaning against a corral fence. It was a picture taken before she was sick. It was the way Carolyn wanted to remember her.

She imagined what it would have been like to live in New York with her mother and thought, Mom wouldn't be afraid to talk to strangers. "Trust your instincts about people," is what she would have said. She'd have let me be independent. She would probably have let me take the subway alone.

Tears filled Carolyn's eyes.

"Mom, I hate living with Dad," she whispered to the picture. "It's not like it would be with you. He doesn't let me do anything. I'm afraid I'm going to get just like him, all nervous and scared."

Don't be afraid, her mother's voice rose from deep inside her. *Remember, you're my girl, too. And I'm still with you.*

Carolyn sat perfectly still and continued to listen. But her mother's voice was gone.

A few minutes later, she went into the living room where her father was reading and listening to classical music.

"Dad, I want to take the subway alone," she announced. "I'm old enough."

He closed his book. "That worked out very well with Maya today, didn't it?"

Carolyn nodded. "I'm getting used to the subway. And I know the route to and from the workshop now. I change to the N or the R at Forty-second Street. I get off at Eighth Street. It's really easy." She heard herself sounding like she could do it, but inside she wondered: Can I? "Maya and Joy take the train alone all the time."

"It would be a big help to me if I didn't have to take you back and forth to the workshop," her father said thoughtfully. He marked his place in the book and closed it. "I'll tell you what. As long as you're with Maya, you can take the train. I'll wait with you on the subway platform in the mornings. But coming back, she'll have to walk you back here."

"That's not alone," protested Carolyn.

"New York is a dangerous place and there are a lot of crazies out there," he said.

The image of Newspaper Boy flashed in Carolyn's mind. Is _he_ a crazy? she wondered.

"You haven't lived in the city all your life like Maya and Joy," he continued. "Though, frankly, I'm not sure I'd approve of anyone your age running around this city alone."

"But —" Carolyn began.

"Either you take the train with Maya or I have to bring you back and forth," he said firmly. "Of course, I'll have to discuss it with her myself."

Ideas toppled over one another in Carolyn's mind. All she had wanted was to be able to take the subway alone. And now her father was going to ask Maya to go back and forth to the workshop with her. How would Maya feel about that?

Forty-six blocks uptown, Maya was taking pictures of her three sisters. Shana sat on the couch, flipping through a magazine, waiting for Maya to finish so they could go to meet up with Delores and Jay-Cee.

Maya wanted to photograph her sisters in natural poses, not all smiles for the camera. Nine-year-old Hannah was braiding five-year-old Naomi's hair. Piper, who was three, was building a house of wooden blocks at Naomi's feet. A perfect shot, thought Maya.

She squatted and framed the shot through the lens.

"Hey, Piper," Shana called out. "Look up. Sister's taking your picture. Smile, pretty girl."

Maya lowered the camera and turned to Shana. "I'm trying to take a *candid* shot."

"If Pipe's head is down, how are you going to see her face?" Shana protested. "She's so cute."

Maya groaned. "Sha-na! I'm the one taking the picture."

Shana thought for a second. "But —"

"You're being bossy, Shana," Hannah put in. "Right, Maya?"

"Ye-eess," answered Maya. She raised an eyebrow at Shana. "What do *you* think? Are you bossy?"

The phone rang.

"Saved by the bell," exclaimed Shana.

While Maya answered the phone, she saw Shana pick up her camera.

"Come on, Pipe," Shana cooed. "Give Shanny a big smile."

Piper smiling up at Shana. Hannah scowling. Naomi crossing her eyes and sticking out her tongue. Click.

"Perfect," said Shana. She turned to Maya. "That is exactly what each of your sisters is like."

Hannah and Naomi pleaded with Shana to take a better picture of them. "Me, too. Me, too," added Piper.

Maya — still on the phone — held her finger to her lips to tell them all to shush. "Yes, Mr. Kuhlberg," she said. "I guess. I mean sure."

On the other end, Mr. Kuhlberg gave her directions about how to meet Carolyn at the 79th Street stop.

"Okay. I'll be there at nine-fifteen."

Mr. Kuhlberg asked her if she wanted to talk to Carolyn again.

"No, that's all right, just tell her bye. Yes, I will. You have a nice weekend, too."

Maya hit END CALL.

"What was that all about?" asked Shana.

"Nothing," answered Maya. She didn't want to tell Shana she'd become Carolyn's keeper. Shana would say she was letting white people use her. "Hey, Shana, what were you doing with my camera. Huh?" she said to change the subject.

Shana came over to Maya, pushed her on the couch, and put her arms on either side of her so she couldn't escape. "I might be the bossy one, but you're turning into the girl with all the secrets. Who is Mr. Kuhl-whatever. You got yourself a baby-sitting job or you got a job-job? Tell."

Maya tried to duck under Shana's right armpit, but that exit was closed. And now her sisters had joined forces with Shana. Hannah grabbed her ankles. Naomi tickled her ribs. Piper was climbing on her head.

"Stop!" shouted Maya. "I give — I give up."

The little girls slowed down but did not stop. Maya and Shana locked eyes. "Baby-sitting. Sort of. There's this girl in the workshop. Her name's Carolyn. Her father asked me to go back and forth to class on the subway with her." She laughed. "Can you believe it?"

"How old is she?" asked Shana.

"Our age. I guess. It's so weird. I mean it's like I'm baby-sitting her."

"Why'd you say yes?"

"I wish I hadn't." She grabbed both of Naomi's hands in her own to stop the tickle torture. "Carolyn is from way out West someplace. She's like this country girl who doesn't have a clue about living in the city."

Hannah and Naomi went back to hair braiding. Piper lay on the couch with her head on Maya's lap. Shana sat down beside them.

"This workshop is such bull, Maya," said Shana. "You should have hung uptown with me this summer."

Maya wrapped a black Piper curl around her finger. "It was my grandmother's idea."

"Josie said it was in the stars that you should take pictures with white girls all summer?" asked Shana. "Sounds to me like the stars are plain stupid."

Joy was finally at her mother's. She finally had privacy. No silly Sue. No baby-sitting cranky Jake. She held her camera out at arm's length with the lens facing her, faked a surprised expression, and pressed the button.

Checking the shot in the viewfinder, she saw that she'd shot only her mouth and neck. Need to hold the camera a little higher, she decided. On the third try, she had the shot she wanted. She fed the image into Photoshop. Next, she brought up the image of her father holding up baby Jake. She deleted Jake's face and pasted hers in. There.

Joy had no memories of her father playing with her when she was little. Once, when her father and Sue didn't know she was listening, she'd heard him say, "I didn't spend that much time with Joy when she was little. I was always on the road or working late. I'm going to do it right with Jake."

No wonder I don't remember him playing with me, she thought. He didn't.

Joy studied the image on the monitor — her head on baby Jake's body. Her father grinning up at her. I won't be showing this one to the class, she thought. Still, she dropped the photo into a file and saved it as "Collage 1." She went to the bureau mirror and studied her reflection. Her father was always saying what fabulous hair she had. Sue said it was her "best feature." Well, I'm sick of it, she thought. It's hot. It's in my face all the time. She pulled her hair back to see what she'd look like without it. I'm going to have it all cut off, she decided. What would Sue and her father think? she wondered. Her mother, she knew, would be glad. She'd been after her all year to shorten her hair. Joy grinned mischievously at her reflection and thought, I might even like it. Or I might not, she thought as she turned from the mirror and let her hair drop. Who cares?

As the train pulled into Eighth Street on Monday morning, Maya felt excited, nervous, and a little silly about leaving a note for Newspaper Boy.

"Maybe he won't even be here," Carolyn said in her ear as they left the subway car.

"Maybe," agreed Maya.

The two girls walked to the trash can without looking around.

Maya put the paper on top.

They turned and walked up the stairs.

Halfway up, Carolyn looked back and saw Newspaper Boy heading toward the trash can. He is so cute, she thought. Even cuter than I remember.

"He took it," she told Maya. "He almost missed the train."

The two girls exchanged a smile and ran up the rest of the stairs and out of the station. As they crossed Third Avenue, they spotted Joy at the food stand.

"Newspaper Boy took the paper," Carolyn blurted out.

"Great," Joy said with satisfaction. "Let's think up another note for Thursday."

They walked side by side to the media center.

"I have an idea," said Maya. "How about: Did you?"

"Did you?" repeated Joy. "That's perfect."

"Did you — what?" asked Carolyn.

"Did you . . . whatever," answered Maya. "It's open-ended. It could mean 'Did you . . . have a nice day?' or anything he wants it to mean."

"Did you brush your teeth this morning?" added Joy. "Did you have a — I don't know — bagel this morning?"

Is that supposed to be funny? wondered Carolyn. Or is it irony? But she didn't ask.

"We better hurry," said Maya, "or we'll all be late."

Joy enjoyed the business about Newspaper Boy, but she wished she wasn't going to another boring workshop session. She changed her mind when she walked into the basement room. Ten large color photos were posted along one wall. They were photos of newborn babies — every one of them looking surprised or frightened. They were the ugliest baby pictures Joy had ever seen and she absolutely loved them.

Maya stared at the photos in amazement. She remembered seeing Piper only a few minutes after she was born. She'd looked like one of those babies. Wrinkled and a little squished.

Carolyn remembered the newborn colts and fillies on the ranch — all wet and awkward.

"Take a seat, everyone," instructed Beth. "I'm interested to hear what you have to say about these photos."

Maya, Carolyn, and Joy sat in the three seats nearest them. Maya glanced in Charlene and Latifa's direction. They couldn't care less where I sit, she thought.

Charlene pointed out that some of the newborns looked like old people.

"Birth and death," said Beth. "Closely related."

"How come they're so ugly?" asked one of the boys.

"What's ugly?" asked Beth.

"I think they're interesting and real," said Joy.

"We're used to some advertiser's vision of babyness," added Maya. "All cute and soft and perfect."

"I was trying to show what it's really like to be newborn," added Beth. She pointed to a squinting, wrinkle-faced newborn. His tiny hands batted the air. "That's my son, Michael."

"Did you take that picture yourself?" asked Charlene. "I mean right after you just — like — uh — had him."

"I did," answered Beth. "That photo started this project."

At the end of the workshop session, Maya went up to Beth and told her that she loved the photographs and thanked her for bringing them in. Carolyn waited for her. She hoped that Maya would suggest they do their next assignment — Where do you live? — together.

"Let's go," Maya told Carolyn as she led the way to the door. "I have to get uptown."

Joy walked to the Village after the workshop and went into a hair salon called HAIR. She'd gone by it a hundred times, but today she was going in for a 1:30 appointment with a guy named Chad.

Brian, Chad's assistant, washed her hair and led her, towel-topped, to Chad's chair.

"My, this is wonderful thick hair," cooed Brian as he combed it out. "Lucky you."

Joy's stomach flipped and her heartbeat picked

up speed. Did she dare to have all that "wonderful thick hair" cut off?

Chad appeared over her right shoulder, brandishing his scissors like a sword. "So you're Joy," he said. "What can we do for you today?"

She met his bored gaze in the mirror. "I'd like it cut short. Very short."

His eyebrows arched. "Really," he said with sudden enthusiasm. He put down the scissors and folded her hair up under itself. Peering at the result in the mirror, he murmured, "Yes, yes. I think so." He drew a line with his finger at the top of her neck. "How about this length? With that wonderful square jaw you could pull it off."

With my fat face, you mean, thought Joy. Still, she said, "All right. That'd be okay."

"And how about having the hair off the face on the top and sides? Short, a little layering would do it."

"Whatever," she said, looking down so she wouldn't have to look at herself anymore. A tumble of wet hair fell over her face.

Chad pulled the long tresses up and ran his fingers through them as if to say good-bye.

Then. *Snip. Snip.*

Joy stared at the pile of her discarded hair mounting on the floor.

Brian's legs appeared beside Chad's.

"My, aren't we brave!" he exclaimed.

She still didn't look up.

Snip. Snip.

"Up with the head, Joy," Chad directed.

Joy finally raised her head. Chad's eyes met hers in the mirror. "Don't look so worried," he scolded.

She watched as he finished off the cut and blew it dry. He handed her the mirror and swiveled her around to see it from all sides.

"You have great structure," he said, the tips of his fingers grazing her jawbone. He put his face next to hers and smiled at their reflection. "Do we like it?"

Maybe my jaw *is* square, thought Joy. She tried a little smile. It grew bigger. "We do," she agreed. "Thanks."

"Nice cut," said the receptionist as she settled Joy's bill. She glanced at Joy's oversized blouse. "A new cut calls for new clothes."

As Joy walked down Sixth Avenue, she caught her reflection in a store window. Her clothes looked too big below her trimmed-down hair.

A few minutes later, she was in a boutique trying on lightweight blue jeans and a short-sleeved red T-shirt.

"The red works great with your complexion and dark hair," said a clerk who was as old as her grandmother. "I love it on you. But do me a favor, sweetheart, try a size down."

Joy changed into the smaller size the woman gave her and checked her reflection in the dressing room mirror. She'd never worn anything that showed her breasts before. She felt a little naked. But, on the other hand, with the tighter clothes she didn't think that she looked so fat. This is me, she thought. This is who I am. She grinned at her own reflection. I'm doing a makeover on my own. Not with those fashion-police girls from my school. Not with my mom. Not with Sue.

Joy was back in her room at her mother's when she heard the front door open. "Hello. Hello," called her mother. "You here, honey?"

Joy walked down the hall toward the kitchen. What if her mother hated her haircut? Well, I don't care, she thought. It's my hair.

Her mother was emptying a bag onto the kitchen counter. "I got us a roast chicken and a pasta salad for dinner," she reported without turning around.

Joy simply said, "Hi."

Her mother glanced over her shoulder and gave out a little scream of fright. "I — I didn't recognize you," she stuttered. "What have you done?"

"Got a haircut," answered Joy, a lump rising in her throat. "I just decided . . ."

"I always said you'd look great with short hair," her mother said matter-of-factly. "I was right."

Joy swallowed the lump.

Her mother turned back to unpacking their take-out dinner.

Carolyn looked out of each of the four windows in their apartment. The two in the main room faced 82nd Street. One in each of the bedrooms faced the yellow brick wall. Carolyn thought of all the interesting sights in her new neighborhood that you couldn't see from the apartment. The American Museum of Natural History with its towers that made it look like a castle, the boat basin on the Hudson River, Strawberry Fields in Central Park, loads of interesting stores on Columbus Avenue. It would be so much fun to spend a day just wandering around shooting pictures of her new neighborhood. She'd have a double set printed up so she could send some to her grandparents and some to Mandy. But how could she take pictures if she couldn't leave the apartment? She didn't want to do it with her father. He would make her too nervous. And she wouldn't ask Maya because she was already stuck taking her to the workshop. But what about Joy?

Carolyn pulled the workshop participants list out of her backpack and found Joy's number. Fear rolled through her stomach. She glanced at the photo of her mother smiling out at her and thought, Mom, you wouldn't have been afraid to make a simple phone call.

She picked up the phone.

Joy was trying on the summer clothes she had at her mother's. The purple linen pants and top were too baggy. She had to get some new clothes. But where? She had a Bloomingdale's charge card. But she hated Bloomingdale's, with all their trendy clothes and skinny shoppers. The image of REMEMBER ME flashed in her mind. It would be really fun to shop there. Her cell phone rang. She flipped it open and saw that the call was from Kuhlberg. "Hi, Carolyn," she said.

"I wondered if you wanted to do the assignment together tomorrow?" Carolyn blurted out. "I mean, if you're not busy and — uh — if you want to."

"What was the assignment again?" asked Joy as she turned from the mirror.

"About where we live — our neighborhoods, I guess. Do you have to take pictures of both your neighborhoods? I mean where you live with your mother and then where you live with your father?" I sound so stupid, she thought.

"Well, I'm certainly not doing twice the work because I live in two places, if that's what you mean," said Joy flatly. The breeze from the open window blew on Joy's newly bare neck. It felt good. Her head felt lighter, too. She wondered how many pounds her hair had weighed. "I'll take pictures up here, around my mother's. Where I am now."

With her free hand, Joy flipped through the remaining tops in her closet. All large or extra large. Maybe Carolyn would go uptown with her to Remember Me. She certainly wouldn't ask hip Maya to do it. But Carolyn might do it just to have someone to hang out with. "I have an idea," she told Carolyn.

A few minutes later, Carolyn put down the phone. "Yippee," she yelled, running from her room.

Her father looked over his laptop screen and smiled. "I haven't heard that from you in a long time."

"Joy and I are going to take pictures together tomorrow," she said. "And go shopping. Can I?"

Her father looked alarmed. "Is she picking you up and bringing you back? No traveling alone."

"I know," she said. "She's picking me up here. It was her idea."

Harlem

Maya walked into the school yard. A guy with a red scarf tied low on his forehead was shooting baskets with a taller guy with shoulder-length braids.

"Can I take some pictures of you guys playing?" Maya called out.

The tall one grinned as he ran past with the ball. "Am I so pretty?"

"Uh-uh," she teased back. "I'm looking for ugly."

Maya moved around with the players and pointed the camera up.

Braids bouncing. Long sleek brown legs in motion. Ball in the air. Click.

Maya squatted.

Red Scarf dribbles the ball. Click.

Maya stepped up on a bench.

Braids steals the ball and runs to the basket for a jump shot. Click.

Maya ran with the players.

Click. Click. Click.

Sweat beaded on her forehead. This is like dancing, she thought. Me and Grandpa's camera and the boys from the 'hood — all moving together.

She finished the roll of film. "Thanks, guys," she shouted.

"Make me famous, babe," shouted the tall man.

"Cover of *Sports Illustrated*," she called back over her shoulder.

She left the school yard and reloaded her camera.

A block later, Maya noticed a man and woman in business suits leaving a storefront real estate office. Colorful advertisements for sales and rentals dotted the front window.

She held up the camera. "Can I take your picture? It's for a summer workshop project. I'm photographing my neighborhood."

"Sure, little sister," the man said. His bright blue tie was the same color as the sky behind him.

"I like your tie," she said. *Click.*

The woman pointing to the sign over the front door — RENAISSANCE REALTY — *and smiling for the camera. Click.*

After a couple of blocks of looking for what to shoot next, Maya stopped in front of the corner grocery. She looked over the open crates of fruits and vegetables. So many shades of green, orange, red, and yellow in orderly rows.

Close-up of peaches. Click.

Blushing apricots next to the green grapes. A peek of red pepper at the upper edge of the frame. Click.

The owner, old Mr. Rodriguez, came out carrying a white bucket of bright yellow sunflowers. Maya greeted him with a hi.

"Josephine's granddaughter," he said, recognizing her. "Your grandfather also took pictures of my fruit and flowers."

A pleasant chill ran through Maya. "This is my grandpa's camera."

What did Grandpa's photos of fruits and flowers look like? she wondered as she walked away.

Three blocks later, Maya stopped in front of an empty wreck of a building. Sunlight danced off the sheet metal covering the windows. A drugged-out dude — his head dropped to his chest — nodded and twitched the day away.

Maya looked up and down the block. There were other abandoned buildings. I shouldn't be walking around here alone, she thought — especially with a valuable camera. But this is my neighborhood, too. I want to photograph it.

She crossed the street and set up a long shot.
Derelict building and drug addict. Click.

A hand on her shoulder. "Whatja think you're doin'?"

Maya's heart skipped a beat as she stood up and swung around. *My camera could be a weapon,* flashed through her mind.

Camera raised, she faced Delores. Shana and Jay-Cee were beside her.

"Whoa!" Maya said, lowering the camera. "I almost hit you."

Delores backed away, hands up. "You gonna *shoot* me?" she teased.

"Girl, what are you doing shooting pictures of no-good drug addicts when you could be helping me with my career?" asked Jay-Cee. She struck a haughty model pose in her stretch miniskirt and halter top.

"I thought you were meeting us, girl," scolded Delores, her hands on her hips.

"Would you all stop calling me girl? You know I hate that," protested Maya.

"Get over it, *girl*," teased Delores.

Shana took Maya's arm. "Come on. We're getting pizza. I'll help you take pictures after."

Maya dropped her camera in her backpack and the four girls walked arm in arm toward Broadway, breaking only to let people by. Someone — a white girl coming from the other direction — waved to them. Red hair. Only one person I know with that hair, thought Maya. But what's Carolyn doing up here? And who's she with?

By the time the girls met, Maya knew who it was. She dropped her arm link with Shana and De-lores.

"Joy!" Maya shouted. "Your hair! It's so — so great. I didn't recognize you."

"Don't you love it?" said Carolyn excitedly.

Maya looked around at her real friends. Delores, with her hands on her hips, was showing attitude. Shana was whispering something to Jay-Cee.

Remembering her manners, Maya introduced

Carolyn and Joy to everyone else. Jay-Cee said hello friendly enough, but Delores and Shana barely mumbled a hi.

Silence.

Maya doesn't want us up here, crossed back and forth across Joy's mind.

"Was I supposed to meet you or something?" Maya asked Joy and Carolyn. "Because I'm busy."

"No-o-o," answered Joy.

Carolyn shifted nervously from foot to foot. "We're going to your mother's store," she blurted out. "To shop. Joy wants to get things to go with —"

"Whatever," interrupted Joy, walking past Maya and her friends. "We've got to go."

Maya was annoyed with Joy. What did she think? That a person would just drop everything to go shopping with her? But she didn't want to hurt Carolyn's feelings. So she yelled after them, "Have a nice day."

Carolyn looked over her shoulder, made a little wave, and called bye.

Joy didn't look back. Carolyn doesn't even know when people are making fun of her, she thought.

Shana shoved Maya's shoulder. "Have a nice day!" she mimicked sarcastically.

"You turning into some kind of downtown girl, Maya?" asked Delores.

"It was a *joke*," Maya snapped. "What happened to your sense of humor?"

"What happened to yours?" Shana shot back.

They went into the crowded pizza parlor, sat at a table toward the front, and ordered a pie with pepperoni.

"That girl with the red hair," said Delores. "What's with the accent?"

"That sure wasn't *south* she was talking," added Jay-Cee in her put-on deep southern accent.

Maya told them a little bit about Carolyn and Joy. But she didn't tell them a thing — not a thing — about Newspaper Boy.

"And what's the big deal about that girl Joy's haircut?" asked Shana.

"I didn't think it was so great," added Jay-Cee.

"What'd she look like before?" wondered Delores.

"Worse," answered Maya. She suddenly realized that Joy had been wearing jeans and a tight T-shirt. And she'd looked good in them. A lot better than she did in all that baggy black linen. What kind of clothes will she pick out at my mother's? Maya wondered. She suddenly wished that she could be in two places at once.

Carolyn took a short denim skirt from a rack of clothes. Mrs. Johnson was going through the rack ahead of her.

Joy came out of the dressing room in a pair of dark brown Capri pants and a short orange V-necked top.

"Wow," exclaimed Carolyn. "That looks great on you."

Joy checked her image in the mirror. "It's okay," she said as if she didn't care. Meanwhile, her heart was racing to the beat of *I like it. I like it. I like it.* Carolyn, smiling, met her reflected gaze. Embarrassed, Joy looked away.

An hour later, Mrs. Johnson rang up their purchases. Carolyn bought the denim skirt and a pink sundress with black piping, for a total of ten dollars. Joy had a whole new summer wardrobe for less than a hundred dollars.

"I'll tell Maya you were here," Mrs. Johnson called after them as they were leaving.

"Like Maya cares," mumbled Joy.

Joy's right, Carolyn thought, Maya doesn't care.

A cell phone rang. Carolyn, thinking it was Joy's, looked at her.

"It's yours," Joy told her.

Carolyn tucked the Remember Me shopping bag under her arm and plunged her hand into the small bag slung over her shoulder. The blinking, ringing phone was under her camera. She opened it. There was only one person who would call her.

"Hi, Dad," she said.

"Where are you?" he asked, scolding. "You were supposed to call me."

"I'm —" She looked for the closest street sign. "At a Hundred and Twenty-fifth Street."

"I thought you were taking pictures in the neighborhood," he exclaimed. "I've been looking all over for you."

A feeling of dread and panic seized Carolyn. Had something happened to one of her grandparents? "Is something wrong?" she asked.

"Yes, something is wrong," he said with angry emphasis. "I can't trust my daughter. You were supposed to stay in the neighborhood and you were supposed to ask permission if you wanted to go anywhere else."

When Carolyn finally ended the conversation with her father, she told Joy, "I've got to go home. I'm grounded for the rest of the weekend."

The two girls headed toward the subway stop. "Your dad's awfully strict," Joy sympathized.

Carolyn nodded. A familiar, horrible thought started to grow in her mind. She tried to shove it back, like always. It was an evil thought. Wicked. No one should have a choice of who would die. And if God had given her that choice, she couldn't have said take my father, just — please, please, please don't let my mother die.

Her father was waiting for her when she walked into the apartment. "I'm sorry I yelled at you" were the first words he said. "We really need to have a talk." He looked around. "Sit down, honey."

She did.

He sat in a chair facing her.

Carolyn studied her hands and picked nervously at a fingernail. "I'm sorry I didn't call you, Dad," she said. "I forgot."

She glanced up at the kitchen clock. It was six

o'clock on Friday. She was grounded until Monday. Did that mean she couldn't leave the apartment at all — even with him?

"I can't have you running all over the city," he said slowly. He hesitated. "Listen, Carolyn, I think I may have made a mistake bringing you to New York City. I've decided that when the photography workshop is over, you should move back with your grandparents. You'll go to school with your old friends."

Surprised, she looked up at him. "Why? Because I forgot to call you today?"

"It's more than that," he answered. "You're just too young to be on your own here. But you're too old for a baby-sitter, which I can't afford, anyway. I worry about you all the time. I have to work again this weekend. I'll have to travel in the fall."

He'll be glad to get rid of me, Carolyn thought. I'm too much trouble. Well, I don't like living with him, either.

"I think you'll be happier," he added.

"Okay," she agreed.

He looked at the floor and was silent.

The phone rang. Is it for me? Carolyn wondered. Does being grounded mean I can't talk on the phone?

But the call was for her father.

She took her shopping bag to the bedroom. Her father hadn't even asked what she'd bought. He doesn't care, she thought. She hung the dress and skirt next to the winter jacket she'd brought from Wyoming. Soon she'd be putting her clothes back in her suitcase. Soon she'd be going home.

She remembered the line "If I can make it there, I'll make it anywhere." Well, I haven't, she thought.

Joy unlocked the front door of her father's apartment and carried her suitcase into the living room. Sue came in from her bedroom and screeched, "Look at you! Your hair! Just gorgeous. Totally gorgeous." Her gaze wandered down Joy's body. "I like the new clothes, too. You did a real makeover. And without me, you naughty girl." Hugging Joy, Sue added, "Just kidding. But, seriously, if you want to go on a diet, I can help you. And you haven't done anything about makeup. I can help you with that, too."

If you don't shut up, I'm going to scream, thought Joy. She picked up her suitcase. "I have to put my stuff away."

The door to the apartment opened and her father walked in with a bouquet of red roses in his hand and Jake in a child carrier on his back. He handed the roses to Sue. "From your boys," he said proudly. He turned and saw Joy. His eyes, she noticed, bulged with surprise. "Joy! What did you do to your hair?"

"Doesn't she look *gorgeous*, Ted?" Sue enthused. "All grown up. She doesn't look so — it makes her look a lot thinner."

"But what happened to my baby?" he asked, still staring at her.

"I'm not your baby anymore," Joy tried to tell her father. But he didn't hear her because baby Jake had taken one look at her and started howling.

Sue assured Jake that it was just his big sister looking extra pretty.

Her father's attention was focused on the crying baby, too.

Joy took her suitcase to her room. It was going to be a long, boring weekend.

The number 1 train pulled into 79th Street at 9:32 on Monday morning. Maya leaned out the door, spotted Carolyn on the platform, and shouted her name. Carolyn made it into the car before the doors closed. Her father, Maya noticed, watched until the subway pulled away. Looking around, Maya saw that she'd lost her seat on the train — again. The two girls stood facing each other in the crush of people who'd entered the subway car with Carolyn.

"Hi," said Carolyn shyly. "Thanks for meeting me." Since the day she'd gone shopping with Joy in Harlem, Maya had seemed cold to Carolyn. They weren't even talking much in the workshop and never did anything together after class — except take the train together. They hadn't left any new messages for Newspaper Boy, either. Which was okay, since they didn't even see him anymore. Where did he go? Carolyn wondered. Maya had said he probably thought their little notes were childish. Joy had said that his schedule probably changed.

The train came into the 72nd Street stop. Carolyn shifted her backpack closer to her body to make room for the people getting on. As the train pulled out of the station, she thought about asking Maya if she had a nice weekend, but stopped herself. That would sound too much like "Have a nice day."

Maya caught her eye and smiled. "Did you have a nice weekend?"

It's like she read my mind just then, thought Carolyn. The train lurched forward. "My weekend was okay," she answered, even though the weekend had been boring and lonely. Except for Friday night. "There was this jazz band at the museum," she told Maya. "We went to that. My dad likes jazz."

"Did you take pictures of them playing?"

"I didn't think of it," admitted Carolyn. "But I didn't have my camera with me anyway. And it was dark — I don't think they'd let me use a flash. Did *you* have a nice weekend?

Maya's face lit up. "It was great. I went to a concert, too. Hip-hop. In the park. A whole bunch of us went. I shot two rolls of film." Maya felt sorry for Carolyn with that strict, boring father, so she didn't tell her any more about the fun things she'd done on the weekend. She pulled the newspaper out of her backpack with her free hand. "Do you want part of the paper?"

Carolyn shook her head. Her father had instructed her not to read on the train. "Always be on the alert," he'd warned her.

They changed trains at 42nd Street. Carolyn rushed to keep up with Maya. They went upstairs, through a tunnel, downstairs, up another set of stairs, and finally down some more stairs before reaching the platform for the N and the R trains.

"I wonder if we'll see Newspaper Boy today," Carolyn said when they were finally on the train.

"Maybe," said Maya as she pulled out her paper again. "I really don't care."

I do, thought Carolyn.

By the time they reached the Eighth Street stop, Maya had read all of the newspaper that she was interested in, so she put it on the trash can as usual. Carolyn looked around. No sign of Newspaper Boy. She followed Maya up the stairs to the street. When Carolyn reached the top step, she looked back. He was there, on the platform, smiling up at her. She smiled back. Was he looking for me? she wondered. Or was he looking for Maya?

"You're okay, girl," Joy heard behind her. "Looking go-o-d."

Glancing over her shoulder Joy saw Incense Man smiling at her. "Uh-huh," he added appreciatively.

As Joy continued down the street toward the media center she stood a little taller. Looking good. A guy had never said that to her before. Another thought rolled in. Only three weeks ago Incense Man had called her a cow. She felt angry at him again, but she wasn't sure why.

"Joy!" shouted another voice. Carolyn. Joy waited for her. While she'd been avoiding Maya since they bumped into her in Harlem, she was beginning to think she liked Carolyn. Even if she did act a little young sometimes.

"I saw Newspaper Boy," Carolyn blurted out when she and Maya had reached Joy. "Here's the strange thing" — she turned to Maya — "I didn't tell you this yet. He didn't have any metal on his face. It was all gone!"

"How did he look?" asked Joy.

"Naked," answered Carolyn.

Maya and Joy laughed. Joy was still smiling as she walked into the workshop room. The smile fell when she saw the photos that were displayed around the room. Big photos of a very old, very sick-looking woman. In one photo, she was in a wheelchair. In another, being helped into bed. Then sleeping with her mouth open. Laughing. Crying.

Maya scanned the two walls of images, too. "They're all pictures of the same old woman," she whispered to Carolyn.

Carolyn was staring at the photo of the old woman in a hospital bed, a respirator covering the lower half of her face. In her mind's eye she saw her own mother — her thin, ill mother just days before she died — a respirator cupped over her nose and mouth. I could never have taken a picture of my mother like that, she thought. It's too scary and sad. Had Beth taken them? Who was the woman?

"Did you take these pictures, Beth?" Maya called out.

"Yes," answered Beth. "They're of my great-aunt Louise during the last year of her life."

"Why did you take them?" asked Latifa. "They're sort of gross."

"No they're not," argued Maya. "They're honest. She looked at death the way she looked at birth. Realistically."

"That doesn't mean it isn't gross," protested Latifa.

Beth pointed to the photo closest to her. It was a close-up of the old woman's face — all lines and wrinkles. "Look at the twinkle in her eyes," she said. "Even when she was very sick, she was still full of life."

The more they looked at Beth's photos and talked about them, the more Maya liked them. She was glad when Beth assigned them to spend the next two weeks doing a photo portrait of one person.

When the class was over, Joy told Carolyn, "I don't like to photograph people. I may just have to skip this assignment."

Carolyn slipped her notebook into her backpack. She'd already picked a subject. She'd written it down. MAYA'S GRANDMOTHER — JOSIE. But how do I ask her? she wondered. Should I ask Maya first? What if Maya wants to photograph Josie?

"Hold it, everyone," Beth called out. "I forgot to tell you something."

The time-to-go chatter halted and the people already on their way out turned toward Beth.

"We're having a photo exhibit at the end of the

workshop," she said. "Friday, August sixteenth, from six to eight."

A couple of kids mumbled protests.

"Where?" called out Charlene.

"Right here. We'll set up this room as a gallery. You can invite people — your parents, friends, whoever. Everyone in the workshop will display pictures." She looked right at Joy when she repeated, *"Everyone."*

Who's going to care about my stupid pictures? wondered Joy.

"One last thing," added Beth. "Think about having a couple of your favorite shots blown up. We'll talk about it all next session. Now get out of here."

Maya and Carolyn got seats on the N train going uptown. As it plunged through the tunnel between Eighth and Fourteenth streets, Maya thought about the portrait assignment. She'd ask Shana to be her subject. It might help them get close again. Jay-Cee would be jealous. But model wanna-be Jay-Cee wasn't right for the natural candid shots she would do. As the train pulled out of the 34th Street station, Maya realized that Carolyn had just asked her a question. She turned to her. "What'd you say?"

"Do you know who you're going to photograph for that portait assignment?" Carolyn asked.

Maya nodded. "My friend Shana. You met her."

The train pulled into 42nd Street. Maya stood up. Time to change trains.

*   *   *

It was Friday night and Joy was baby-sitting. She sat on the living room floor with Jake. Their father picked him up for a hug good-bye. "You have all the emergency numbers, Joy," he said. "We'll call you during intermission." He put Jake back down and straightened up. "You two have a good time together."

Jake whimpered.

"He's teething, poor baby," cooed Sue. She waved at Jake. "Bye, my darling."

Sue didn't pick him up for a good-bye, thought Joy, because she's afraid he might mess up her fancy dress and thick makeup.

"There's a teething ring in the freezer," Sue called from the doorway. "If he gets cranky, try that."

The door closed, the lock turned, and they were gone. Off to their theater date, leaving her alone with Jake — again.

Two minutes later he was squalling.

Joy picked him up and walked around the room. He still cried.

"Please, stop," she pleaded. "I can't stand it."

He stopped, looked at her, and let out an ear-shattering *Whahh!*

"If you're going to cry anyway, I might as well put you back down," she scolded. She laid him on his stomach on the floor so he could crawl. He rolled onto his back. *Whahh!*

Joy leaned over and looked him in the eye. "They all think you're so cute. But you really look quite ugly right now." He stopped crying and stared back at her. "And frankly, when you eat — you make a big mess. Quite disgusting." He was still listening, so she continued. "There are cute pictures of you all over the apartment, but that's not how you usually look." She picked him up. "I have an idea. I'll show you how you really look."

Whahh!

"Okay. Okay. I'll get you that teething thing first."

Joy took the cold teething ring out of the freezer, gave it to Jake, and carried him into her bedroom. She had a subject for the portrait assignment.

"Stop posing. I might as well be taking pictures of Jay-Cee," scolded Maya. She'd been shooting Shana in Shana's apartment for more than an hour. "You're acting all phony in front of the camera."

"Take pictures of me when I'm working," suggested Shana. "You know. At the camp with the kids."

"I already had that idea," said Maya.

"Will you take pictures of the kids, too?" Shana asked. "And give them some? They'd love that."

"Yeah, yeah," agreed Maya. "If you just stop acting so phony."

"All right!" *Shana grinning, her hand raised for a high five. Click.*

On Sunday, Maya, Shana, Delores, and Jay-Cee went to Riverside Park. Lots of their friends were there. Someone brought a boom box. Maya took pictures of Shana as she danced around. Fooled around. Played with a Frisbee.

After shooting for a while, Maya lay on a blanket and looked up at the clouds floating behind the leafy green treetops. An image flashed in her mind. Carolyn in her room, making a phone call. Why did she just pop into my mind like that? she wondered. Delores dropped down beside her. "How those white girlfriends doin'?"

"I dunno," answered Maya. "That's their business, not mine."

When Maya got home, her mother shouted for her to come to the kitchen and help with dinner. "Carolyn called you," she said, handing Maya a bag of carrots. "You're doing salad, but you can call her back first."

Piper ran over and grabbed Maya's leg. "Up. Up," she pleaded. Maya lifted her up, gave her a carrot, and went to find the phone.

"Hi," she said when Carolyn answered. "What's up?"

"I was wondering," said Carolyn, "if I could do that portrait assignment about your grandmother. I guess I'd have to come home with you someday if she says yes. If you think she'd let me. I mean, if you don't mind."

Josie would make a great subject, and Carolyn doesn't have anyone else to photograph, thought Maya. "I'll give you her phone number. You can ask her yourself."

Carolyn hung up the phone and glanced at the photo of her mother. *I know, Mom. Don't be so shy. Josie's a nice lady. Just call her.*

An hour later, Josie was sitting next to Maya at Sunday dinner. "Your friend Carolyn wants to take my picture," she said as she passed the potatoes to Maya.

"Is that okay?" asked Maya. "I mean that I gave her your number?"

"Yes, of course," answered Josie. "Carolyn interests me."

"She's taking *your* picture, Grandma." Maya laughed. "Not the other way around."

Josie put her hand over Maya's and looked into her eyes. Uh-oh, thought Maya, Grandma's getting one of her ideas. "Watch out for Carolyn," she said thoughtfully. "I'm worried about her."

Piper pulled on Maya's arm. "Cut it. Cut it. Mama said."

Maya turned her attention to the piece of chicken on her sister's plate, but her grandmother's warning repeated in her head: "Watch out for Carolyn. I'm worried about her."

Q Train

When Maya walked to the 125th Street station on Monday morning, it was hot and steamy on the street but a good deal cooler on the elevated subway platform. She was wondering if it was going to be another hundred-degree day when she noticed Shana and her day campers waiting for a train, too. More staff and campers in bright orange T-shirts dotted the platform. Shana, in a white T-shirt that read STAFF, saw Maya and waved to her.

Maya went over to Shana and her group. "Where you guys going?"

"The zoo," shouted Shana over the rattle and roar of an approaching number 1 train.

"We're getting off at 59th Street," added a little girl wearing bright pink eyeglasses.

The subway car doors opened and they all got on.

"We're gonna see the polar bears!" bragged a boy. "And puffins. Lots of puffins. Shana showed us pictures."

Shana held on to the boy with one hand and grabbed the pole with the other.

This is a chance to get some candid shots of Shana, thought Maya. She reached into her bag for the camera.

Carolyn and her father stood side by side on the 79th Street subway platform. He glanced at his watch, looked at her, and announced, "I have a seminar at ten o'clock." He looked at his watch again.

She hated how he was always checking the time. It's a nervous habit, she decided, like the way he's always clicking the top of his ballpoint pen.

"You can go, Dad," she said. "Maya will be here any minute."

Checking his watch again. "All right, then, I think I'll be going." Looking around the platform. "Stay back, away from the edge. And call me when you get to your class."

"I'll be fine, Dad," she insisted. "Don't worry."

He patted her on the shoulder and left.

He'll be glad when I'm in Wyoming and he doesn't have to worry about me anymore, she thought. And I'll be glad when I don't have to worry about him worrying about me.

The underground air was thick with damp heat and bad smells. A train approached the station. Carolyn moved a few feet forward and looked quickly up and down at the open doors. Lots of people got off, but not Maya. A man carrying a big box grumbled at her to get out of the way. The doors closed.

As the train pulled out of the station, Carolyn

saw Maya through a subway car window. She isn't even looking for me, Carolyn realized with a jolt. She's left me alone on the subway platform. She snubbed me.

Maya held on to the pole with one hand and raised her camera with the other.

Shana telling two girls to stop pushing each other. Click.

Shana brushing strands of loose hair off another girl's forehead. Click.

More candid shots of Shana with the day campers. Click. Click. Click.

The train moved smoothly along the tracks. "What's the next stop?" Maya asked Shana.

"Seventy-second Street."

Carolyn! thought Maya. I forgot to pick up Carolyn.

The girl wearing pink glasses pulled on Maya's shorts and grinned up at her.

"Take *my* picture."

"I can't," Maya said as she slipped the camera back into her backpack. "I have to get off at the next stop."

"I thought your class was in the East Village," said Shana.

"I meet Carolyn at 79th Street. You know, that red-head from the workshop," Maya reminded Shana. "I have to go back. It's a major pain."

Shana rolled her eyes. "Right. The unpaid baby-sitting job."

"Please, please, please take my picture," the little girl pleaded.

"Take my picture, too," said one of the boys.

"Me, too," said the boy next to him.

"I'll take everybody's picture," agreed Maya. "But not now. Will you be back at Kids' Place this afternoon?"

"Yes!" said the three kids in unison.

"We'll be there by two-thirty," answered Shana.

"I'll be there."

The train pulled into the 72nd Street station. The door opened. Maya smiled around at the children. "I'll come by this afternoon and take *everybody's* picture," she said.

"Promise?" asked the pigtailed girl.

"Promise," Maya called over her shoulder.

"Yay!" she heard the kids yell as she stepped out of the train.

The dirty heat of the subway station engulfed her. If Carolyn isn't waiting for me, she thought, I am going to be majorly pissed.

A downtown train pulled into the 79th Street station. Carolyn got on. I can get to the workshop on my own, she thought as she held on to a hand-crowded pole. I can take care of myself.

The train lurched forward.

She watched through the window as the train rolled in and out of 72nd Street, 66th Street, 59th Street.

At 50th Street, she noticed a woman in a bright purple sundress and green straw hat. She looks like an eggplant, thought Carolyn. She sneaked another look. The woman was staring back at her. Carolyn looked away. Don't make eye contact with anyone, her father had warned.

The train pulled into 42nd Street.

Time to change to the N or the R, Carolyn reminded herself. Just follow the signs.

In the rush of passengers getting off the train, Eggplant Woman stayed right beside her. Carolyn pulled her backpack around to her front and held it to her chest as she went up a flight of stairs. The woman kept step with her.

Down a set of stairs.

Eggplant Woman walked beside her through the tunnel connecting the train platforms. Carolyn could feel her eyes on her.

Everyone moving quickly — eyes straight ahead. Carolyn speeded up.

The woman speeded up, too.

Carolyn changed her bag to the other side and walked faster.

"Your hair is amazing," the woman murmured. "I'd kill for hair that color. Is it natural?"

Kill? Carolyn broke into a run, weaving in and out of the fast-walking commuters.

Up a few steps. Down some more.

There was a train at the platform, doors open. The man in front of her was running to catch it. I can make it, too, she thought. She stepped into the subway car as the doors were closing.

Why did I run away from that woman? Carolyn wondered as she reached for an overhead rail. She just asked me a question about my hair. But maybe she's one of those pickpockets who work in teams. Her father had told her about them. One thief spills something on you — like a soda. Or just bumps into you. Or asks you a question. While you're distracted, the second thief steals your bag. Usually by cutting the strap.

The train pulled into the next station. Doors opened. More people got on. Shoving, pushing. Carolyn moved farther into the subway car, trying to find a rail or pole to hold on to.

She felt proud of herself. She'd done it. She'd taken the train alone. And it wasn't like she disobeyed her father. It was Maya's fault for not meeting her.

The train pulled into the next station. Carolyn got off and faced a sign that read: CANAL STREET. This wasn't her stop.

In two big steps, she was back on the subway car.

The doors closed behind her.

The old train lurched forward, almost throwing her into a man's lap. She grabbed for a rail overhead to steady herself.

"Sid-down," the man commanded in a gravelly voice.

She lunged across the aisle and fell-sat into an empty seat.

There were a lot of empty seats on this train now. The sign on the top of the window said it was the Q train. Q?

As the train rumbled on, the only thought in Carolyn's head became *I'm on the wrong train. I'm on the wrong train.*

Sunlight suddenly filled the car. Through the dust-streaked windows she saw the hazy blue summer sky.

Carolyn's heart pounded as the train went *clickity-clack* over a bridge. She looked down at the water and wondered, *Where is this train taking me?*

It went back underground. She sneaked a look around the subway car to check out the other passengers. Could one of them help her?

Who can I trust?

There were two Asian women with plastic grocery bags talking to each other in a singsong language. Chinese?

Three young men with toolboxes were speaking in another language she didn't recognize. Russian?

A frazzled-looking mother with a big beach bag and three young children. The oldest put an empty sand pail on a smaller child's head. He howled. The woman scolded them in what sounded to Carolyn like Spanish.

The train pulled into a station. DeKalb. Where was that?

Carolyn swallowed the lump in her throat. Her heart pounded.

Don't cry. Think about what to do.

Atlantic Avenue. The three men got off. Four teenage boys got on.

Carolyn sat down again and held her backpack to her chest. *I'm lost!* screamed in her brain.

The train stopped at Seventh Avenue, Prospect Park, and then Church Avenue.

Carolyn looked around and spotted a big square of blue subway map behind the rowdy boys.

I have to wait until they get off to look at it. If they get off.

One of the boys returned her glance and pursed his lips in a kiss-kiss. She looked away. They were aboveground again, on a bridge that spanned a neighborhood of houses and stores.

Maybe it will turn around when it reaches the end of the line. Then I can ride back and go home. But the train didn't turn around. Not at Kings Highway or Neck Road or at Sheepshead Bay or Brighton Beach.

The boys got off at Brighton Beach.

Beach? I never heard of a beach in New York City.

There was only one person left in the car besides her. The man who told her to sit down.

The train bumped and clacked on the aboveground tracks. Carolyn, her body swaying with the subway car, went over to the map and studied the colored lines of the subway routes. The lines wavered out of focus.

I must not cry.

Another stop: Ocean Parkway.

Carolyn's vision cleared and she followed the yellow line of the Q train with her finger. According to the map, she wasn't in Manhattan anymore. She was in Brooklyn. The train was slowing down.

West Eighth Street and Surf Avenue. Eighth Street? But not the Eighth Street she needed. She looked out the window. A roller coaster came into view. And the biggest Ferris wheel she'd ever seen. And beyond these rides, she saw water that went on as far as she could see. And waves.

The train screeched to a stop.

The man stood and was coming toward her. He was huge. "Get off," he growled. "This is the end of the line." He stared down at her. "You lost or something?"

"No," she managed to say. "This is where I'm going."

She rushed off the train and moved quickly through the crowd down the long, noisy tunnel. What if that man followed her?

She was on the street.

To her right, there were rides and sideshows and a road leading to the water. To her left, a street of shops and food stalls.

Keep walking — fast.

She passed open-air shops spewing clingy smells of fried food and loud music and lots of people on the move.

Is he following me?

She snuck a look over her shoulder and didn't see him.

Her cell phone rang.

My father. What will I tell him?

A tear-choking lump rose up in her throat as she opened the phone.

"Hello," she croaked.

"Look, Carolyn, I'm sorry I forgot to get you this morning. I missed the stop and went back for you. You should have waited." It wasn't her father. It was Maya. "I'm sorry you missed class and everything. I suppose your father is furious at me."

"I'm lost," Carolyn whispered into the phone. "I — I don't know where I am. I don't know how to get home."

"What do you mean?" asked Maya. "What happened?"

"I took the wrong train. I'm on some kind of island. There're rides here. Big ones. And the ocean, I think."

A man with a zillion tattoos walked by arm in arm with a woman with even more. A guy with a big boom box on his shoulder, rap music blaring, pushed past her.

She couldn't hear what Maya said over the music. She saw the man from the subway coming up the block toward her. She ducked into a restaurant and looked for the sign for the rest room.

At the other end of the phone connection, Maya and Joy were in the rest room at the media center.

"What's happening?" Joy asked Maya.

"I think she's in Coney Island. All I can hear now is a lot of noise." She handed the phone to Joy.

"Hello? Hello? Carolyn, it's Joy," she said.

"There's this man," Carolyn whispered into the phone. "He was on the train. I just saw him again. I don't know what to do."

"We'll come get you."

"It'll take you a long time." Carolyn sobbed. "Besides, I don't even know where I am."

In an emergency the first rule is to stay calm, Joy reminded herself. "Maya said you could see rides and the ocean. Did you see a big roller coaster?"

"Yes," answered Carolyn. "I saw it from the train, too."

"Is the roller coaster called the Cyclone?" asked Joy.

"That's what the sign said," Carolyn said, remembering.

"I know where that is," Joy assured her.

"Wait for us at the roller coaster. We'll leave right now." Joy looked at Maya, who nodded in agreement. "Try to stay calm," Joy continued. "We're on our way. Okay?"

"Okay," said Carolyn in a small, frightened voice.

Joy closed her phone.

"Should we tell Beth?" Maya wondered out loud.

Joy shook her head. "She might tell Carolyn's father. Let's just go. So what if we cut the rest of the class? We have to get Carolyn."

They left the rest room, the building, and the neighborhood and headed out to Coney Island.

Carolyn went into the rest room stall and let the tears finally come.

She still felt frightened.

What should I do until they come? What if they can't find me?

When she came out, two women with big hair, small clothes, and spiked-heel shoes were leaning toward the mirror, putting on makeup. Carolyn splashed cold water on her own tearstained face.

"Look at that girl's red hair," the taller of the two women said to her friend. She drew a dark line on her lower eyelid.

"I bet that hair glows in the dark," said the other woman. She dabbed aqua sparkle on her eyelid. "Uh-huh."

"You want your hair that color, honey?" the taller woman said. "I could do it."

Carolyn left the bathroom. That was the second time a stranger had mentioned her hair. It gave her the creeps.

I'll go to the door of the restaurant. If I see Subway Man, I'll stay inside and order a soda or something.

"Hey, Red," shouted the bartender. "Rest rooms are for customers only." He pointed to a sign. "Can't you read?" It wasn't a restaurant. It was a bar.

"Sorry," mumbled Carolyn.

A couple of guys at the bar laughed. Another said, "Leave her alone, Mikey. She's just a kid."

Carolyn rushed out of the bar and checked both ways. No sign of Subway Man.

Looking up, she spotted the giant, snaking roller coaster. The Cyclone.

She crossed the street and headed into the crowded amusement park.

Scratchy music blared from a loudspeaker. People were walking in all directions. Some toward the beach that was beyond the amusement park. Others — eating while they walked — checked out the games or lined up to go on rides.

DANTE'S INFERNO read the sign over a fun house. A devil with a twisting reptile tail hung over the entrance. His huge mouth wide open in an evil grin. It was so scary and ugly that she couldn't help staring at it.

"Come on in, little lady," said the man selling tickets. "It's hell. It's swell."

She shook her head no as she backed away from him and turned. *Thunk.* She'd bumped into a big guy behind her, sending his hot dog to the ground and a stream of yellow mustard dripping down the front of her white polo shirt.

"Oh, man!" shouted the guy. He was, she saw, with three other boys — all big, tough-looking teenagers.

"Make her pay for it," said one of them.

"Maybe she wants you to clean the front of that shirt for her," said another, laughing.

She turned and ran. Their laughter was behind her. Were they following?

To her right she saw a trailer with a sign reading: LADIES' ROOM. She ran up the ramp.

"Hey, hold on," said a man with a change apron around his waist. "Quarter."

She reached into her backpack for change and for the second time escaped to a rest room.

Will those guys be waiting for me when I go back out? What if that guy had tried to wipe the mustard off my chest?

Her phone rang. Joy, she thought as she opened the phone. Joy would tell her what to do.

Carolyn opened the phone and said, "I'm so scared. These guys —"

"Carolyn, what are you talking about?" her father exclaimed, panic rising in his voice. "Where are you?"

Coney Island

Should I tell my dad that I took the train alone and got lost? Carolyn wondered.

Mom, what would you do?

Carolyn closed her eyes for a split second and felt the answer.

"Sorry, Dad," she said into the phone. "I thought you were Joy." She was surprised at how calm her voice sounded. "I was playing a joke on her."

"Are you sure you're all right?" he asked. Nervousness hung at the edges of the question.

"I'm fine, Dad. We're in Coney Island. Taking pictures. For the workshop. It's — a — field trip."

"Why didn't you tell me you had a field trip today?" he asked.

"It was kind of a last-minute thing," she explained. "Then we had to take the subway to get here. We sort of just got here."

"Call me when you're leaving there," he instructed. "Tell me again where you are."

"Coney Island," she said, keeping her voice bright and cheerful. "There are all these rides, and the ocean is here. I've never seen the ocean. It's really cool."

"*Cool*?" he said. "Can't you find a more precise word than that?"

"It's *beautiful*. And vast. The ocean is *vast*."

"That's better," he said. "I look forward to seeing your pictures, honey. And stick with your group. That was a foolish joke you were playing on your friend. But we'll talk more about that tonight."

He really has no idea what kind of trouble I've gotten myself into, she thought as she closed the phone.

Two women and their children came into the rest room. One of the boys was crying over a dropped ice-cream cone. Carolyn looked down at the bright yellow mustard stain splashed across the front of her polo shirt and went to the sink to try to clean it off.

I didn't tell Dad the truth, she thought. But Mom wouldn't have, either. Like when Tailgate was spooked by a mountain lion and threw her. Tailgate was okay, but Mom was laid up for a week with an injured knee. Mom said it was a good thing that Dad was out of town. Mom never told him about the accident. He was also out of town when Mandy and I ran away on our ponies. Mandy's mother wouldn't let us have a sleepover to celebrate the last day of first grade, so we ran away. Carolyn smiled to herself, remembering the ponies geared up with their rolled-up *Little Mermaid* sleeping bags and the saddlebags packed with everything they thought they needed for living on their own — including a large bag of candy.

"Don't tell your father about this," her mother had warned when she found them in the canyon a few hours later.

Carolyn rubbed at the mustard stain with a wet paper towel. It wasn't coming out.

We didn't really lie to Dad those times, she decided. There are just things you don't tell him. He's always so worried about safety. He even thought I was too young to have a pony. Well, I wasn't. And that day in the canyon, Mandy and I weren't lost. We knew exactly where we were and we could have gotten home on our own — if we wanted to. So why was I such a scaredy-cat today? I should have just gotten off the subway and asked the person in the booth for help. And those loudmouthed boys and the guy on the subway? Mom wouldn't let people like that frighten her. Mom could take care of herself. And so can I.

Carolyn studied her reflection in the mirror. Flaming red hair, yellow mustard stain on her shirt. If I see those guys again, I don't want them to recognize me, she thought.

She went into her backpack and pulled out sunglasses and a dark green baseball cap with the ranch's Diamond D insignia. After she put on the glasses and tucked her hair into the cap, she looked at her reflection again. Better. Except for the shirt.

When Carolyn left the rest room trailer, she went

into the first shop that sold T-shirts. She had a twenty-dollar bill in her wallet for emergencies. Well, this is an emergency, she decided. She picked out a blue T-shirt with CONEY ISLAND written above a drawing of the Cyclone. As she changed shirts in the dressing cubicle, she wondered if she'd dare ride that roller coaster. Would Maya and Joy want to do it? She and Mandy always went on the roller coaster at the county fair. But that roller coaster was about one-tenth the size of the Cyclone. She checked her watch. Forty minutes had passed since Joy said they were coming for her — she'd better go over there. She'd already paid for the T-shirt and was out of the store when she went back in to buy a roll of film. Her father expected to see pictures.

A cop car cruised slowly up the street. I could ask those cops for help, she thought. But I don't need help now. My friends are coming to meet me.

Three children and their parents passed her. "I'm going to stay in the water *all day*," the little boy told his father.

"Me, too," said the father.

The mother looked back at Carolyn as she passed her. "I love your T-shirt. Where'd you get it?"

Carolyn pointed across the street. "At the store on the corner. They had lots. In white, too."

"Thanks," said the woman.

Carolyn hoped Maya and Joy would want to go to the beach. She'd never stood at the edge of the ocean.

When Carolyn passed Dante's Inferno, the man out front didn't even notice her. Later, she'd take a picture of that devil sign. What had she been so afraid of? A mountain lion on the trail was something to be afraid of. Not a stupid picture of a devil with a snake tail.

She loaded her camera and took five shots of the roller coaster.

Her phone rang.

This time she checked the readout to see who was calling before speaking. It wasn't her father.

"Hi," she said.

"It's us," said Joy. "We're here. Where are you?"

"At the roller coaster," answered Carolyn.

"So are we," said Joy.

Carolyn turned around and came face-to-face with Joy and Maya. Maya hugged her.

"We didn't recognize you," said Joy. "We were looking for red hair."

"Where'd the shirt come from?' asked Maya. "It's cool the way the roller coaster goes around to the back."

"I just bought it," explained Carolyn. "Some guy spilled mustard all over the front of my shirt. I had to change." Suddenly, she was embarrassed by her fears. "Being here was so scary at first. And I really panicked about the subway. I'm sorry you left the workshop and everything just to come get me."

Maya patted her arm. "We're just glad you're okay."

"It was a boring class, anyway," added Joy. She looked around. "I've never been here before. It's wild."

"I've never seen the ocean — any ocean," said Carolyn. "I mean before today." She smiled.

"You're kidding! We used to come here when I was little," said Maya. "I was afraid to go on the roller coaster."

"I've never been on a roller coaster," Joy admitted.

"Do you want to do it now?" asked Carolyn. "I mean, since we're already here."

It'd be kind of fun, thought Maya. "Sure," she said. "Joy?"

"I'll do it," agreed Joy — even though her stomach turned flips just looking at the roller coaster.

"We could have lunch and sit on the beach, too," said Maya.

"We better do the roller coaster before we eat," commented Joy.

"Or we'll all barf," added Maya. She took out her camera. "I'll take pictures."

"Of us barfing?" teased Carolyn.

"Yuck!" exclaimed Maya.

"That's disgusting!" Joy laughed.

Maya and Carolyn exchanged a grin. Joy's laugh was deep and rolling and wonderful. They'd never heard it before.

Carolyn and Joy before the roller coaster ride. Click.

Carolyn and Joy flushed and exhilarated after the ride. Click.

"I'm hoarse from screaming," croaked Joy when their roller-coaster car jolted to a stop. "I loved it!"

A wide grin across Joy's face. Click.

They got hot dogs, french fries, and sodas from the food stand on the boardwalk and sat on a bench facing the water to eat.

Carolyn told them about the subway ride and all the things that scared her and how the man tried to get her to go into Dante's Inferno fun house — the Tunnel of Hell.

"Want to do it?" asked Maya.

"No!" cried Joy and Carolyn in unison.

As they were finishing up the fries, Carolyn told them about her father's phone call and that she'd lied to him about coming to Coney Island. Then she told them about running away with Mandy and how, after that, her mother took her and Mandy on a three-day riding and camping trip. How they'd slept under the stars in the mountains. "That was a long time before my mother got sick," Carolyn concluded.

Joy wondered if Carolyn ever wished her father died instead of her mother. "You must miss your mother a lot," she said softly. "She sounds like a great mom."

Carolyn looked at her lap and whispered, "She was."

Maya jumped up. "Let's go down to the water." She grabbed Carolyn's hand. "Come on."

They took off their shoes and walked across the sandy beach to the ocean.

Thin lines of whitecaps broke at the shore. The water was dotted with sunbathers.

"Let's go in," suggested Maya.

"We don't have bathing suits," said Joy. She held up her shoes. "And we have all our stuff."

"I've never been in the ocean," said Carolyn. She looked up. The sun was still high in the sky and it was a very hot day. "Our clothes would dry."

"Give me your backpacks and shoes," instructed Maya. "I'll find someone to watch them." She scanned the sunbathers closest to the water. Two elderly women in beach chairs were smiling at her. She went over to them.

"Such a hot day," one of them commented.

"Do you want us to watch your things so you can go in the water?" asked the other.

"That'd be great," answered Maya.

Carolyn ran into the water yelling, "The last one in is a rotten egg!"

Maya squealed as the water hit her belly.

Joy dove in.

Carolyn surfaced, with water streaming down her face. "It's salty!" she screamed.

Joy came up for air and looked back at Maya and Carolyn. Maya's dark skin glistened in the sunlight. Carolyn's hair was truly flame-red with glints of gold. They were both laughing. I'd love to take their picture just like that, she thought.

After swimming, the three friends went for a walk on the beach. When they came back, the two women lent them their towels so they could lie down in the sand.

They laid the two big beach towels side by side so all three of them could fit.

Joy lay back and closed her eyes. She felt like she was still floating in the ocean. The sun's warmth seeped into her skin, and she drifted off into a half sleep.

Carolyn lay on her stomach, listening to the waves and feeling the sun drying her new T-shirt. She wondered if her shorts would dry before she got home. She needed to take more pictures to show her dad. She'd write to Mandy and tell her about the roller coaster. And wasn't the sound of the waves beautiful? *Slap, lap, slap.* Had her mother ever been to the ocean? She'd ask her grandmother that sometime. *Slap, lap, slap.* And the smell of ocean air and the sound of the waves. *Slap, lap, slap.* And she was asleep.

Maya lay on her back, eyes closed. Joy and Carolyn weren't so bad. In fact, they were pretty cool. She was having fun with them. Carolyn had been really frightened, but in the end she'd overcome her fears. She was brave and adventurous. Maya wondered how brave and adventurous *she'd* be in Wyoming. And even though Joy was grumpy sometimes, she could be funny. Shana didn't understand that it was important to get to know all kinds of people from all kinds of backgrounds. Shana! Maya squinted to read her watch. 3:00. She'd said she'd take pictures of the day camp kids. She'd promised. Even if she left now, she wouldn't be at Kids' Place until after four. Besides, her clothes were still wet. How could she explain all this to Shana?

Maya sat up and looked out at the sea. I want to be friends with Maya and Carolyn, she thought. But I don't want to lose my old friends.

On the subway ride home, Carolyn sat between Maya and Joy. Except for the waistbands of Joy's skirt and Carolyn's shorts, their clothes were completely dry.

Carolyn turned to Joy. "Who are you going to photograph for the portrait assignment?"

"My half brother. But he's a baby, so he's not very interesting." She shrugged. "Whatever."

"But that's so cute that you're taking pictures of him," said Carolyn.

Joy frowned. "Not really. I'm catching him in those ugly-baby moments. I don't particularly like him. Well, it's not him. It's not his fault. My father and his wife — they call me their 'built-in baby-sitter.' I hate it!" Joy realized she'd never told anyone how much that bothered her before — not even her mother.

"Welcome to the club," said Maya. "I'm always having to watch my sisters. My parents have been calling me 'Little Mama' since I was four."

The train pulled into the Kings Highway station.

"Who are you taking pictures of for the portraits?" Joy asked Maya.

"Her friend Shana," Carolyn answered for Maya. She turned to her. "Right?"

The subway went into a short tunnel and out again. "I'm not so sure I want to use the pictures I took of Shana," said Maya. "But I don't know who to do." She didn't tell Carolyn and Joy that Shana would be furious at her for standing up the day camp kids. Or that Shana was angry with her for hanging around with two white girls.

"I think you should take pictures of Newspaper Boy," said Joy. "We could write him another note saying you want to photograph him." She looked from Maya to Joy. "Don't you think?"

"Yes!" answered Carolyn excitedly.

"No way!" said Maya.

Eight subway stops later, Maya agreed.

By the time they reached 79th Street, they'd composed a note.

I AM TAKING A PHOTOGRAPHY WORKSHOP AT THE YOUTH MEDIA CENTER. ONE OF OUR ASSIGNMENTS IS TO PHOTOGRAPH A PERSON. COULD I PHOTOGRAPH YOU? IF YOU SAY YES, I COULD DO IT AT 8TH STREET. HOW ABOUT ON MONDAY BEFORE YOU TAKE THE TRAIN? TWO FRIENDS WILL BE WITH ME, BUT I'LL BE THE ONLY ONE TAKING YOUR PICTURE.

Joy said she'd walk Carolyn home, so Maya didn't have to get off the train. "I don't know if I'm going to leave that note," Maya told Carolyn and Joy before the subway doors separated them from her.

At home, Maya had a phone message from Shana. She was furious. "You don't promise kids something and not deliver," she said. "Or maybe *you* do."

Maya picked up the phone to call Shana back. I should at least try to explain, she thought. And I have to make it up to those kids. But she put the phone down without calling. It was better to give Shana time to cool off.

Carolyn was in the kitchen washing lettuce for a salad. The doorbell rang and a key turned in the lock. She knew it was her father. He liked to warn her that he was coming in so he wouldn't frighten her.

"It's me," he said when he walked in.

"I know, Dad," she replied. "I started the salad."

While they made dinner together, he asked her about the field trip to Coney Island.

"I took pictures of the roller coaster," she said. "Then we went on it. It was awesome."

"*Awesome?*" he repeated. "Is that precise?"

Why couldn't he just let her talk without correcting her all the time? "I think it's precise. Being on that roller coaster filled me with *awe*. But I wouldn't say it was *awe-full,* so it's *awe-some.*"

He smiled over at her. "Well said." He carefully turned the turkey burgers over. "So what else did you do?"

She told him about the ocean and some of the other pictures she'd taken. But she skipped the part about taking the subway alone, swimming in her clothes, and letting strangers watch her backpack.

He put a burger on a roll for her. "I'm glad you

had a chance to go to a famous New York site while you're still here."

She flipped open the ketchup bottle top. "While you're still here" rang in her ears. He can't wait to get rid of me, she thought. He's my own father and he doesn't even want to live with me.

Thursday morning, Maya didn't forget to look for Carolyn at 79th Street. The two girls found seats and squeezed in next to each other.

"Are you leaving Newspaper Boy the note?" asked Carolyn.

Maya nodded. "I feel a little stupid doing it, but now I really want to photograph him."

"Is it still okay if I photograph your grandmother this afternoon?" asked Carolyn.

"Of course," answered Maya. "She's making you lunch."

Carolyn hoped they'd eat in the garden. That's where she mostly wanted to photograph Josie. She'd ask her to do what she usually did in the garden, like pick flowers or weed. "Try to forget I'm here," she'd say.

"I'm going to take pictures of kids from this day camp in my neighborhood this afternoon," Maya was saying. "But I'll still take you home. Gran said you could hang out with her till I get back."

"I wish I could take the subway home alone," said Carolyn.

"And to Coney Island?" teased Maya.

"Next time, I thought I'd go to Staten Island," Carolyn teased back. "Then I could go on a boat, too."

Carolyn was behind Maya when they got off the train at Eighth Street, but she was the first to spot Newspaper Boy. "He's coming toward us," she hissed in Maya's ear.

Maya walked nonchalantly over to the trash can. A hand reached out and picked up the newspaper as soon as she put it down.

"Thank you," said Newspaper Boy.

"You're welcome," said Maya, looking up.

His blue eyes, Carolyn noticed, sparkled. So did the metal that was back on his face.

"Sorry about all the notes," said Maya.

"I like," he said. And he was gone — into the subway train with the newspaper.

Joy walked to the media center on the far side of the street. She didn't want to pass Incense Man. She didn't want him looking at her and making comments about how good she looked. It made her angry and at the same time it gave her the creeps.

A whistle rang out from across the street — the kind you make by putting both middle fingers at the corner of your mouth. Joy ignored it and kept walking.

"Joy," shouted Maya.

Turning, Joy saw that it was Carolyn whistling. She smiled to herself. Carolyn is such a cowgirl, she thought as she crossed the street to meet them.

After the workshop, the three girls walked side by side toward the subway station. "How will Newspaper Boy let you know if you can photograph him?" Carolyn wondered out loud.

"I suppose he'll just be there Monday morning," said Maya. "Anyway, I have plenty of photos of Shana if he doesn't want to do it."

Joy was the first to see the message posted on the lamppost outside the subway stop.

After that, Maya spotted one on the telephone booth.

Then Carolyn noticed one on the subway stairwell.

They were all photocopies of a note made up of cutout newspaper headline letters. CAMERA GIRL. OKAY. MEET YOU AT NINE O'CLOCK ON FRIDAY. SERGE

Upper West Side

Josie welcomed Carolyn and invited her in. They brought chicken salad sandwiches and a pitcher of iced mint tea out to the garden and sat at a round table under an umbrella. "So, Carolyn, your birthday is August second," observed Josie as she poured the tea. "That's this Saturday."

Carolyn, her mouth full of sandwich, nodded. She was surprised that Josie remembered the exact day of her birthday.

"You're a Leo," continued Josie. "Leos shine in the world. You are full of fire and spirit."

"I am?" said Carolyn, surprised.

Josie patted her hand. "I know you haven't been feeling that way lately, dear. But you will feel your light again soon." She brushed a fly off the table. "So tell me about Wyoming."

As they ate, Carolyn told Josie about the ranch, her mother, and the horses. When they'd finished lunch, Josie led her around the small garden and talked about her plants.

Carolyn wondered when she'd be photographing Josie.

"So where would you like me for those pictures?" Josie asked suddenly.

"I'd like to start here," answered Carolyn. "In your favorite place in the garden. If that's okay with you."

Josie lying in the hammock, looking up at the sky. Click.

Josie pruning the roses. Click.

Close-up of Josie laughing. Click.

They went inside to see where else Carolyn could take pictures. Josie led her into a little room off the kitchen. The wall facing them was covered, floor to ceiling, with hundreds of names written in neat black script.

"Those are the names of all the students I've taught," she said proudly. "I was an English teacher for forty years and I saved all the class lists."

Josie standing at the desk in front of the names of her former students. Click.

When Carolyn finished the photo shoot, Maya wasn't back.

"I have to prepare an astrological reading for a client," Josie explained to Carolyn. "Would you like to wait for Maya in the garden?"

"Okay," agreed Carolyn. She went back out to the garden and lay in the hammock. She looked up at the clouds moving by and rocked the hammock with her foot. I'm in New York City, she had to remind herself.

Maya took her last shot of Shana's young day campers. She'd taken all of their pictures during a nature walk in Central Park.

"Can I have my picture?" asked a girl who'd followed Maya around for the entire shoot. "Can I have it now?"

"They have to be developed first," explained Maya.

"Line up if you want water," Shana announced.

The children formed a line at the water fountain. Maya, wanting a drink herself, went to the end of the line.

Shana joined her. "After the kids go home, let's drop the film off at the one-hour photo place. Then we'll go look for Delores and Jay-Cee and pick the pictures up later."

"Sorry. I can't. I have to do something else."

"What?" asked Shana.

Maya moved a few steps forward. She didn't want to tell Shana that she had to take Carolyn home. "Something for my photography class. It's no big deal."

"Can you at least get the pictures developed and bring them over in the morning?" asked Shana. "We're taking the kids to Jones Beach. You could come. You don't have that photo workshop on Fridays."

"I'm photographing someone tomorrow. So I can't."

Shana's eyes darkened. "You've changed," she said before turning back to her day campers.

And you haven't, thought Maya as she bent over the water fountain for a drink. If you did, you might be a better friend.

*   *   *

On the way home, Carolyn and Maya dropped off Carolyn's roll of film and picked up the Coney Island pictures. She and Maya sat on a street bench to look at the pictures.

Carolyn laid out three pictures side by side on the bench between them. The roller-coaster car filled with screaming people at the top of the biggest dip. The car in the middle of the dip. And at the end.

"I love these," said Maya. "They're real action photos. You should exhibit them in a row at the show — just like that."

As Maya walked Carolyn to her apartment building, she realized that she wasn't doing it because she'd told Mr. Kuhlberg that she would. She was doing it because she wanted to be with Carolyn.

"I'll meet you on the subway at 8:30 tomorrow," Maya reminded Carolyn when they reached her building. "That's an hour earlier than usual."

"I haven't asked my father yet," admitted Carolyn.

"You *have* to be there when I take Newspaper Boy's picture," said Maya.

"I know," Carolyn told her. "I *will*."

Joy sat at her computer and scanned pictures into her Photoshop program. She needed to fit three images in a postcard-sized space. It would be the front of the invitation for the photography workshop exhibit.

"Joy, you know Photoshop," Beth had announced in front of the class, "so I'd like you to design and print the invitation." Everyone had talked about which photos they should use, but Beth made the final choice. Nerdy Boy Charlie's out-of-focus black-and-white self-portrait. Janice's portrait of her two mothers. Joy's own close-up of a bitten-into jelly doughnut with its bloodred insides spilling out. She wished Maya's and Carolyn's photos were on the invitation, too. She thought they were both better photographers than she was, especially Maya.

Joy was printing out the invitations when her cell phone rang. She was surprised to hear Maya's voice at the other end. They talked about the invitation and the photo shoot of Newspaper Boy the next day.

"We better not call him Newspaper Boy to his face," observed Maya.

"Whatever you say, *Camera Girl*," teased Joy.

They were still talking about the shoot when Maya remembered why she'd called Joy in the first place. "Carolyn's birthday is Saturday. My grandmother told me. She's probably doing something at night with her dad. But during the day, maybe we could do something with her."

Joy spun her chair around and saw herself in the mirror of her closet door. "Does Carolyn know that you know it's her birthday?" she asked Maya.

"I don't think so," she answered. "Let's do something special. It'll be a surprise."

Joy smiled at her mirrored self. It would be fun to pick out a present for Carolyn.

"Excellent!" she told Maya.

By 8:45 Friday morning, Carolyn and Maya were on the N train. "I could hardly sleep last night," Carolyn said. "I kept thinking about all the things I want to know about Newpaper Boy."

"Like what?" asked Maya.

"Like how old he is. And why he has all those piercings. I hope he'll tell us."

Me, too, thought Maya.

Joy waited for Carolyn and Maya at the entrance to the Eighth Street subway. She noticed Serge crossing the street. He stopped on the corner and looked right past her. He doesn't know who I am, Joy realized. Should I introduce myself? She felt herself blushing just thinking about doing that.

A few minutes later, the tops of Carolyn's and Maya's heads appeared below her on the stairs leading out of the subway. She went down a few steps to tell them that Serge was already there.

I hope this guy doesn't turn out to be a major creep, thought Maya as she followed Joy up the stairs. When she reached the street, the sun shone in her eyes so she didn't see Serge. When her vision cleared, he was standing directly in front of her.

"Hello. I am Serge," he announced.

"Hi," she said. "Thanks for — uh — letting me take your picture. I'm Maya." She turned to Carolyn and Joy. "They're in the photo workshop, too." As Serge said hi to Carolyn and Joy, Maya realized she'd forgotten to tell him their names. She hated that she felt so nervous. "This is Carolyn," she added. "And Joy."

"Joy. It is the same like word *happiness*," observed Serge.

What is that accent? wondered Carolyn. Where is he from?

I bet he's from Russia, thought Joy.

Maya took her camera out of her bag.

"I have one question," said Serge. "Why you want to take my picture?"

Maya hesitated, then answered, "Because you're interesting-looking. And the way you kept taking my newspapers — I wondered why. I thought you might be an interesting person, too."

"I read newspapers to learn the new words," he said. "My teacher of English says to do it. And the notes you write in the newspapers — this is fun to read. Everyone in the class, they enjoy." He smiled at Joy. "They en-*joy* this what you write. I show my class. My teacher says, 'Have a nice day' is very American thing to say. In my country we say 'shastlivo,' which means 'good luck.'"

"Where are you from?" asked Carolyn.

"How long have you been in America?" asked Joy, her voice overlapping Carolyn's.

Serge looked from one girl to the other and smiled. "Please. More slowly. It is too difficult with both voices at one time. I don't understand. But it is good to talk to American girls to learn the English. My teacher says to me."

"I have an idea," said Maya. "You can practice your English with Carolyn and Joy while I take your picture. Okay?"

"Why not?" answered Serge.

Serge in close-up — his blond-and-purple hair against the bright blue sky. Click.

The girls learned that he was fifteen years old and that he had come from Moscow in January. He lived with his uncle and his family on Second Avenue, where his uncle was a building superintendent.

Serge standing — legs apart — arms raised in victory. "I love New York," he announced to the sky. Click.

He told the girls that his English classes were in Brighton Beach, which was why he took the train every morning.

A tight close-up of Serge smiling to show off his braces. Click.

They learned that he had the piercings done in a shop in Greenwich Village where he worked — cleaning and running errands. "They want me to have the pierce for the customers to see. I had already one pierce when I came to America." He pointed to the stud in his eyebrow. "This one over the eye. It is American style."

A tight close-up of his eyes. Click.

"That's your eyebrow," said Joy.

"Eye-brow," repeated Serge. "I have only friends

from Russia. I need friends with the English language to learn. My teacher says."

Serge standing between Carolyn and Joy. Everyone smiling. Click.

"It's almost ten o'clock," Carolyn announced. "What time does your class start?"

"Half past ten," he said. "I must to go."

Before they said good-bye to Serge, Joy gave him an invitation to the show. "There will be lots of Americans there," she said. "You can practice your English."

"And see the pictures I took," added Maya.

Carolyn was still thinking about Serge when she walked into her building later that day. Sometimes he was hard to understand, but she'd never met anyone like him. She tried to imagine what it would be like to move to New York and not speak English. What Serge was doing was much harder than what she was doing. The doorman interrupted Carolyn's thoughts by calling out, "A package for you, Miss Kuhlberg." He handed her a box with the Diamond D Ranch return address.

Carolyn took it in the elevator and pressed 10. It's a birthday present from Grandma and Grandpa, she decided.

The elevator doors opened and she got off. Tomorrow she was going to hang out with Maya and Joy. She hadn't told them that it was her birthday. "You're the birthday girl all day," her mother used to say. Tears filled Carolyn's eyes as she unlocked the door to the apartment. It would be her second birthday without her mother.

When Carolyn opened the door to Maya and Joy the next morning they walked in singing "Happy Birthday to you . . ."

When they'd finished singing, Carolyn said all in a rush, "Thank you. Thank you so much. . . . How did you know it was my birthday? Did Josie tell you? Well, it's true . . . it is my birthday!"

"It is," agreed Joy. "All day."

"And we're going to have fun all day!" added Maya.

"To start, I brought bagels, cream cheese, and orange juice," Joy announced, putting a bag on the counter.

"Did your father give you your presents yet?" asked Maya.

"Not yet," she said.

Carolyn got out napkins, plates, and knives. Maya sliced the bagels. Joy poured glasses of orange juice.

"My grandparents sent me a present," Carolyn told them. "It's the most beautiful photo album. They said it's for pictures of when I was in New York City. So I'll always remember my summer here. I'll show it to you." She jumped off the stool. "It's in my bedroom."

Joy put out a hand to stop her. "Whoa, Cowgirl. Hold on. What do you mean *your summer here*?"

"Aren't you going to stay in New York?" added Maya. "I thought you were going to live here now."

Carolyn sat back down. "I'm going back to

Wyoming after the workshop's over," she finally told them. "My dad said I have to. He doesn't want to have to worry about me."

"Did he find out that you took the train alone?" asked Maya.

Carolyn shook her head. "He doesn't even know about that."

"I was going to tell you about my school," said Maya. "My grandmother started it, so you could get in for sure. She said last night that I should tell you about it. It's a really great school. They even wrote about it in the *New York Times*."

Carolyn suddenly realized that Maya did not want her to leave New York.

Joy spread cream cheese on a bagel and muttered, "I guess it'll be more fun in Wyoming with your old friends and the horses and everything."

Joy doesn't want me to go, either, Carolyn realized. She ripped off a piece of bagel and rolled it into a little ball.

Joy looked over at Carolyn. "I can understand if you don't want to live with your dad anymore."

"My dad's okay. Really he is. I think he's just been more nervous about everything since Mom died. I guess it's too hard for him to be the only one responsible for me."

"You're the person responsible for you," said Joy. "You should live where you want. It's your life."

"Do you want to go back to Wyoming?" asked Maya.

Carolyn gave the little ball of bagel a push toward Maya. "I'm getting used to living here. Actually, I like it a lot now. And I know that my mom wanted Dad and me to live together. She told me that."

Maya rolled the bagel ball to Joy.

"You should live where you want," repeated Joy "Period." She squished the bagel ball between her fingers.

Carolyn got home from her birthday-day with her friends at 5:30. So far, she'd had a great birthday. I'm going to have fun tonight with Dad, too, she thought. I'll wear the dress I got at Maya's mother's store and my pony earrings. The boxy purse Joy gave me will be perfect with it.

After she took a shower, she put a photo of Maya and Joy sitting on the beach in Coney Island in the silver frame Maya had given her as a birthday gift. She added it to the collection on her nightstand.

By the time her father came home, she was dressed for her birthday dinner.

"Sorry I'm late," he said as he flipped through the mail. "A researcher is in from Africa and —" He looked up at her and stopped mid-sentence. "What a pretty dress. You look so grown-up."

"Thanks," she said. "I got it at Maya's mother's store."

"When?" he asked. "Why don't I know these things?"

"You were mad at me that night," she answered. "Because I didn't call you when I went uptown."

His eyebrows arched in surprise. "I'm never mad at you, Carolyn," he said simply.

"Well, maybe you were just busy."

"And I'm never too busy for you," he added. "You're my daughter."

If you're not mad at me and you're never too busy for me, why are you sending me back to Wyoming? she wondered. But she didn't say it.

He gave her a kiss on the forehead. "We're going to a restaurant in Central Park. My assistant said it would be perfect for your birthday." He looked at his watch. "Our reservations are at seven-thirty."

When Carolyn saw the restaurant, she agreed that it *was* perfect for a New York City birthday. Their table was on a veranda at the edge of the lake in Central Park. Her view of the lake and trees ended in a row of skyscrapers.

"I haven't gotten you a birthday present yet," her father explained when they were seated. "Because I thought I'd ask you what you want first." He smiled. "So, what would you like as a gift?"

"I don't know," she admitted.

"Think about it. Okay?"

"Okay," she agreed.

Rowboats drifted lazily on the water. Harp music played in the background. The waiter approached with menus. He had a small silver nose ring. When he smiled at her, she noticed a gold stud in his tongue. Her father noticed it, too. When the waiter left he grumbled, "I don't understand why young people have to do that to themselves."

Maybe wanting to do it is enough of a reason, thought Carolyn. But she didn't say it.

After they'd ordered drinks and dinner, Carolyn's father asked her about her day with her friends.

"We had a great time. We walked along the river as far downtown as we could. That's where I called you from. Remember? Then we went to Joy's father's apartment."

He nodded. "Did you like it?"

Even though Carolyn thought that Joy's father's apartment was the coolest apartment she'd ever seen, she described it without once using the word *cool*. She told him that from the big windows in the living room and kitchen you could see the Hudson River and New Jersey and that from Joy's room you could see Ground Zero. But she didn't tell him that when Maya opened the blinds to see what was behind them, Joy burst into tears. Or that Joy had kept her blinds closed since September 11. Or that they'd stood together and looked down at the place where so many had died, and for the first time ever Joy described what she saw that day, and they'd all cried.

The busboy brought them a breadbasket. The waiter brought their drinks.

"And what did you do at Joy's?" her father asked.

She told him how Joy demonstrated Photoshop. But she didn't tell him that they'd scanned in the photos Maya had taken of a guy they'd met at the subway station who had four piercings in his face. Or that they fooled around with the digital images of Newspaper Boy so that he became an old man, a baby, and a woman. And she certainly didn't tell him that she'd laughed so hard when she saw Serge as a big-breasted woman with big blond hair that she thought she'd pee her pants.

The meal at the Boathouse restaurant was delicious and, as the sun set, lights went on in the skyscrapers. Carolyn remembered the long talk she'd had with Joy and Maya about her father.

"Dad," she said, "I know what I want for my birthday."

East Village

The waiter leaned over Carolyn and handed her a dessert menu. "My personal favorite," he said softly, "is the chocolate cake."

Carolyn and her father checked out the menu.

"Chocolate cake is your favorite," her father reminded her. "I wish I'd had time to make you one this year."

Her father always made her birthday cakes and every year — except for last year — she had a big birthday party with a barbecue and chocolate cake.

"Remember when my pony, Jazz, ate the top off the cake?" she asked.

"That was your fifth birthday," he said.

"It was so funny. But I guess it wasn't funny for you, since you made the cake."

"I thought it was hilarious," he agreed. "Seeing Jazz with chocolate all over his muzzle, and the pathetic-looking cake. It sent your mother into a laughing fit, as I recall."

"And you fixed the cake, Dad." Carolyn remembered how he'd scraped off the pony-chewed top layer, covered the damage with whipped cream, and printed HAPPY BIRTHDAY in chocolate chips.

"Actually, the repairs were your mother's idea," he admitted. "I just executed them." He smiled at Carolyn. "You still haven't told me what you want for your birthday. We can go shopping tomorrow."

"My present doesn't cost money," she said.

He leaned forward, interested. But the waiter was back, interrupting them again. Carolyn ordered chocolate cake and another ginger ale. Her father said he'd have the lemon tart and tea.

When the waiter left, Carolyn finally blurted out, "I want to stay in New York and live with you, Dad. I'm not afraid of being in a big city. I'm older now and I can stand on my own two feet. Grandma and Grandpa and Mom used to let me do all sorts of things and I had responsibilities and I learned to be independent. I'll feel like a quitter if I go back so soon." She'd said it all in a rush and had to stop to take a deep breath.

Her father looked out over the lake and didn't say anything.

"So maybe you have to think about it or something?" she added.

When he turned back to her, he had tears in his eyes. "You sounded and . . . and looked so much like your mother just then," he said softly. "All fire and spirit." He paused.

Tears came to her own eyes. "Mom would have wanted us to be together."

"I know," he agreed. "But I believe you're better

off on the ranch with your grandparents than in New York City. They'll be pleased to have you." He smiled hopefully. "This job won't last forever. We can live in our house at the ranch when I'm home, and you'll stay in the big house with your grandparents when I'm not."

"So you've decided for sure?"

He looked her right in the eyes. "You'll be better off in Wyoming."

"Happy birthday to you . . ." Three waiters and one piece of chocolate cake with a sparkler approached their table. Carolyn's father and some other diners joined their voices in the birthday song.

That night she lay in bed wondering, If I'd be better off in Wyoming, why do I feel so sad about leaving New York?

"Hey, lazybones. Get up." Maya opened her eyes. Jay-Cee was hanging over her.

"What are you doing with gold sparkle eye shadow" — Maya glanced at her clock radio — "at ten in the morning?"

"We're going to the beach," Jay-Cee answered. "Get your lazy self ready."

Maya sat up. "You're wearing all that makeup to the beach?"

Jay-Cee checked out her face in the mirror over Maya's bureau. "It's waterproof."

That's not the point, thought Maya. But she didn't bother to say so. Jay-Cee lived in her own model wanna-be glamour world.

"Shana coming?" asked Maya.

"She has a family picnic thing happening today," answered Jay-Cee. She raised her eyebrows at Maya. "Didn't you know that?"

"I was busy yesterday, I didn't see her."

"Well, girl, haul your slow-moving self out of that bed and put on your suit. We want to beat the crowds to Jones Beach."

When Maya came back from the bathroom in her bathing suit, Jay-Cee was holding up the invitation to the photography exhibit. "What's this?"

"For my photography class," explained Maya. "We're having a show."

Jay-Cee pulled a face. "How come I didn't get no invitation?"

"I didn't think you'd want to go," Maya said matter-of-factly. "It's way downtown."

"I go downtown," said Jay-Cee. "It's happening down there. And I *want* to go to your show. Maybe somebody in that class will take my model photos for me." She glowered at Maya. "Since you *would not*."

Maya threw her beach bag on the bed. "I'm officially inviting you, okay? Take a card."

"What about Shana and Delores?"

"Take three cards. I don't care."

"You didn't invite Shana already?" asked Jay-Cee with surprise.

Maya put sunblock and a hair pick in the bag. Her beach towel was already in there. "I told you, I haven't seen Shana. And I'm going to be superbusy getting ready for the show next week. So you just tell her all about it. Okay? But I guarantee you she will *not* want to come."

"Why not?" asked Jay-Cee. "You two are forever best friends."

"It's a long story," said Maya, throwing the beach bag over her shoulder. "Come on."

"Come on, Jake," Joy pleaded. *"Cry."* She was on her knees, ready to take more ugly pictures of Jake for the portrait assignment. Jake — a wide, two-tooth grin across his face — crawled toward her. Her phone rang. She swept Jake up, balanced him on her hip, and ran to answer it. She checked out the caller ID number as she sat on the edge of the bed. "Hi, Mom," she said into the phone.

Jake leaned back against Joy's chest and grabbed at his own feet.

"I got the invitation to your photography show, honey," her mother said. "I have a business dinner thing at eight that evening. So tell your father I'll go to the exhibit on the early side and he should go later."

Joy hadn't seen her parents together since they were divorced when she was six. They hated each other. What bugged her most was that they left it up to her to schedule separate appearances for events they were both expected to attend — like open house night at school.

"Dad wants to come early, too," Joy told her mother, "so they can bring the baby."

"Bring the baby to a photography exhibit?" exclaimed her mother. "Why on earth would he want to do that?"

Jake grabbed the curly telephone cord and put it in his mouth.

She pulled the telephone cord away from Jake. "I don't know, Mom. *You* ask him."

"Well, tell your father that my being at this business dinner is more important than his *baby* attending a photography exhibit."

Jake reached for the telephone cord again. Joy held his hand back. He looked up at her and wailed.

"Mom, I've got to go. I'm baby-sitting."

She hung up the phone and carried crybaby Jake over to the closet door mirror. "Sorry I took the cord from you, but it's not a toy."

She faced him toward the mirror. He looked at himself and stopped crying. Joy studied their reflections, too. They both looked sad.

She patted his little back. "It's okay, Jakey. Your parents aren't divorced." She kissed the top of his head. "I hope, for your sake, they never are."

The baby laid his head on her shoulder. She pulled the camera out of her sweatshirt pocket and aimed it at the mirror. *Click.*

The next Friday, the class met for a special session to bring in their work and hang the show. Before they began, Beth announced, "I want to tell you about a photography workshop I'm offering in the fall. It will be on Saturdays starting in early October."

Carolyn listened to the description of the workshop. They'd be exploring new subjects through photography. And some Saturdays, they'd take field trips to photography exhibits. It sounded cool. She overheard Maya and Joy whisper to each other that they would do it. But I can't, thought Carolyn. I'll be back in Wyoming.

All week, Carolyn had hoped her father would change his mind and let her stay in New York. She'd been cheerful and hadn't complained about having to be taken wherever she went. And she was especially helpful around the apartment. But that morning, he'd told her he'd made a reservation for her to fly back to Wyoming on the following Monday.

"Did you tell Grandma and Grandpa?" she had asked.

He had nodded. "I told them you'd call in the morning."

Carolyn remembered back to her own conversation with her grandparents when her father first said she had to go back to Wyoming. "What do *you* want, honey?" her grandmother had asked. "I don't know," Carolyn had admitted. Before hanging up, her grandfather had said, "Just remember, we always want you with us."

I just wish my father always wanted me with him, she had thought.

The photography show was completely hung by two o'clock.

Joy thought the enlarged photos looked best. She especially liked Maya's blowup of Newspaper Boy, arms outspread, shouting, "I love New York!" That was in the Portraits section. It was Joy's idea that Maya audiotape Serge saying, "I love New York!" Latifa thought they should have lots of different voices saying, "I love New York."

"People could say it in different languages, too," suggested Carolyn.

Latifa, Carolyn, Joy, Maya, and Charles Nerdy-Boy had gone around the Lower East Side recording the voices. They would play it during the exhibit.

Maya stopped in front of Joy's enlarged photograph. She had taken a new photograph for the My Neighborhood assignment. It was the view of Ground Zero from her bedroom window. She'd used Photoshop to overlay a ghostly image of the twin towers on a photo of the empty site. Maya thought it was the most powerful photograph in the exhibit.

Josie was the first person Carolyn saw when she walked into the photo exhibit that evening. While she introduced her father and Josie to each other, she noticed Joy walking in with a woman that Carolyn guessed was Joy's mother. Joy spotted Carolyn and headed toward her. As Carolyn smiled and waved, she overheard her father tell Josie, "The photographs are quite impressive for children."

"They're young adults now," commented Josie. "Shall we take a closer look at them together?"

By the time Carolyn had met Joy's mother, Josie and her father had moved over to the Portrait section of photos. They were looking at Carolyn's blown-up photo of Josie in her garden.

"I better catch up with my dad," Carolyn told Joy. As she approached him from behind, she overheard Josie say, "Why do you think she has to go back to Wyoming?"

Carolyn — not wanting to interrupt — turned around and came face-to-face with Maya's three friends.

"Where's Maya?" she blurted out.

"You should know," answered Shana. "You see her a lot more than we do."

"I do?" said Carolyn, confused. She noticed that the girl, whose name was initials that she couldn't remember, had on spike-heeled sandals. They were the highest heels Carolyn had ever seen on a girl their age. "I like your shoes," she said.

"Thanks," said the girl, smiling. "I got them at Maya's mother's store. I'm Jay-Cee. You're Carolyn. Right?"

Carolyn nodded. "I got my dress there, too."

Jay-Cee checked Carolyn out. "It works for you," she said. "Sweet and innocent-like."

Carolyn didn't know whether Jay-Cee was complimenting her or being sarcastic.

"I'm looking for a photographer for a special project," Jay-Cee continued.

"A special project of self-love," teased Delores.

The hum of conversation in the exhibit rose. More people were arriving by the minute.

"So will you take my model pictures, Carolyn?" Jay-Cee asked.

She shook her head. "Sorry. I'm going home on Monday. Back out west. I was only here for the summer."

"Too bad," commented Shana sarcastically.

"It *is* too bad," Carolyn shot back. "I like living here. People are *so nice*."

Delores poked Shana's arm with her finger and laughed. "She got you, sister."

I was just sarcastic, thought Carolyn proudly. Cool.

Maya spotted Carolyn talking with her friends. If Shana is in one of her uppity moods, she thought, there's no telling what she might say to Carolyn. Maya was moving toward them for a rescue operation when a hand on her shoulder stopped her midstep. She turned around. Serge.

"Hello, Maya," he said formally. "I am here to see the photographs."

First, she noticed that he was in a preppy-boy white shirt and khaki pants. Second, she noticed that he had only one piece of metal in his face — the stud over his eyebrow.

"You didn't have to take the metal off your face," she said.

"It is from respect for meeting the parents," he

said. "My teacher said. And your parents? They are here?"

"Yes, but —" Maya began. The "I love New York" tape interrupted her.

Voices all over the room stopped. Everyone stood where they were, listening to the tape of I love New York. Halfway through, a baby made a happy, loud, shrieking sound. Maya saw that Joy was holding the baby. Carolyn noticed that Joy's mother was gone now and Joy was standing with a man and woman. Her father and stepmother, Carolyn guessed. When the tape was over, everyone applauded and the baby shrieked again, which made the crowd laugh.

"So who should I get to take my pictures?" Jay-Cee asked Carolyn.

"Joy might do it," answered Carolyn. "She's got a digital camera and knows Photoshop. She could make you some cool prints. You met Joy that day in the street. You know, the one with the new haircut."

Jay-Cee wrinkled her nose. "She was snobby."

"She's okay," Carolyn told her.

Jay-Cee left to find Joy.

Carolyn went looking for her father. She found him in front of Joy's large photo of Ground Zero. "This show is very impressive," he told her. "And your friend Maya's grandmother is very interesting. Did you know that she started a school?"

Carolyn nodded. "Maya goes there."

"They have a strong science program and are affiliated with my museum," he said enthusiastically.

"She asked if I'd give a presentation in the fall. If you were staying in New York, that's where I'd send you."

Beth was beside them. Carolyn's father congratulated her on the exhibit and she thanked him. She turned to Carolyn. "I hope you're taking my workshop in the fall, Carolyn."

"I'm going home," Carolyn told her. "I was only here for the summer."

"I'm sorry to hear that," Beth said, looking back to Carolyn's father. "I thought she was going to live in New York with you. I must have misunderstood."

Maya grabbed Carolyn's hand. "I need you," she whispered. Carolyn excused herself and followed Maya.

"What?" she said when they were out of earshot of her father and Beth.

"Let Beth talk to your dad privately," she said. "Maybe she can help."

"Help what?" asked Carolyn.

"Help you stay in New York," answered Maya. "My grandmother already worked on him."

"You told Josie to talk to him about me?" asked Carolyn, surprised.

Maya grinned and nodded. "And Joy told Beth. Now come on, help me entertain Serge."

They looked all over for Serge and finally saw him standing at the snack table with Shana and Delores. Jay-Cee, Carolyn noticed, was deep in a conversation with Joy.

Maya's mother came over to Maya and Carolyn. Maya's little sisters trailed behind her.

"That sundress is perfect for you," Maya's mother told Carolyn. "You should come back to the store. I have a lot of terrific fall and winter clothes."

Carolyn smiled. "Thanks." She didn't feel like saying one more time, "I won't be here. I'm going back to Wyoming."

Her father motioned her to come over to where he stood in front of the My Neighborhood photos.

"You're very popular," he said.

"I am?"

"Everyone I talk to thinks you should stay in New York. Maya's grandmother wants you to go to her school. Beth wants you in her workshop. Did you put them up to it?"

"No, Dad," answered Carolyn. "I didn't." She hoped he wouldn't ask, "Did your friends?"

He looked around the gallery until his gaze stopped at her three-shot series of the roller coaster. "Your photos are very good. I guess I hadn't seen them all." He glanced again at the photo of Josie. "You captured Josephine's spirit."

"Thanks," she said.

"I'm impressed with your friends' work, too," he added. He looked her straight in the eye. "Do you really want to stay in New York and live with me?"

"I do," she answered. "Don't you want to live with me?"

He looked surprised by the question. "Of course I do. You're my daughter. I love you more than anyone in the world. But I worry about . . ."

Her heartbeat speeded up. Her father wasn't trying to get rid of her. He *wanted* to live with her. "I will be safe, Dad. If you let me stay, I promise I'll be careful."

"And follow my rules?"

"Yes."

"I suppose we could try it," he said softly. "Especially since you have a good school to go to and the photography workshop. And you've already made friends."

"So I can stay?"

He nodded. "It's how your mother would have wanted it. It's how I want it."

"Me, too."

"The whole family agrees, then," he said.

She swallowed a lump of tears — a mixture of sadness and happiness that stuck in her throat. She hugged her father. "Oh, thank you, thank you."

Maya — who was nearby with her mother and sisters — saw and ran over.

"Gotta go," Joy told Jay-Cee. She moved toward Carolyn, too.

"I'm staying in New York," Carolyn sang out to Maya and Joy.

The three friends hugged.

Click.

About the Author

Jeanne Betancourt lives and writes in New York City. She has written more than sixty books, including *My Name Is Brain Brian*, *Ten True Animal Rescue Stories*, and the popular Pony Pal series. Jeanne's work has been honored by many Children's Choice Awards. She is also an award-winning scriptwriter and has taught filmmaking to teens.

*You've just finished Three Girls in the City #1?
Now picture this:*

Three Girls
in the City #2:

EXPOSED

★ Carolyn, with a little help from her friends, knows her way around New York now. She has more freedom — and more secrets from her father. When things go bad at Joy's party, Carolyn doesn't tell her dad, and a wall of little white lies grows up between them. Strange thing is, she's got a feeling she's not the only one lying.

★ Maya doesn't want to lose her best, oldest friend, Shana. But Shana is determined to make her choose between old friends and new, and they are both going to lose. Can she make Shana understand that a friendship needs to grow — or go?

★ Joy's changed the way she looks — now she wants to change the way she lives. She's sick of going back and forth between her mom's place uptown and her dad's place downtown. She wants to live uptown with her mom, full-time. Period. She'll be alone a lot but she'll do *what* she wants, *when* she wants. And it will be great, right? Maybe. Maybe not.

Look for Three Girls in the City #2: *Exposed* in stores October 2003

About three girls with cameras sharing good times, worries, brilliant ideas, adventures, hassles, and danger.

Friendship, like the color black, goes with everything.

PRAIRIE RIVER

A JOURNEY OF FAITH

KRISTIANA GREGORY

The year is 1865 and Nessa Clemens is about to turn 14. On her birthday she'll have no choice but to leave the orphanage she's called home for as long as she can remember. Her plan is to escape on the next stagecoach heading west to Prairie River—a town in the middle of nowhere. She doesn't have a job or a home, and she doesn't know anyone, but her faith tells her that everything is going to be all right.

Meet Nessa this June!

www.scholastic.com/books

Available wherever books are sold.

PRT603